DEAD MEN DON'T DRINK VODKA

by

THOMAS E. KRUPOWICZ

TERK BOOKS AND PUBLISHERS

Chicago, Illinois

Copyright 1995 by Thomas E. Krupowicz
All Rights Reserved
Printed in the United States of America

This novel is entirely a work of fiction. Names, characters, places, times and incidents are either the product of the author's imagination or are used fictitiously. Any resemblance to actual events or places or persons, living or dead, is entirely coincidental.

No part of this book may be reproduced or transmitted in any form by any means, electronic or mechanical, including photography, recording, or any information storage or retrieval system, without permission in writing from the author.

Inside cartoon illustrations drawn by **LEO FELTMAN**

ISBN: **1-881690-03-2**

TERK BOOKS & PUBLISHERS
P.O. BOX 160
PALOS HEIGHTS, ILLINOIS 60463

Other books published by **TERK BOOKS & PUBLISHERS**

DEATH DANCED AT THE BOULEVARD BALLROOM
by Thomas E. Krupowicz
ISBN: 1-881690-00-8
12.95

FINGERPRINTS--THE IDENTITY FACTORS
by Thomas E. Krupowicz
ISBN: 1-881690-01-6
39.95

FIRST LINE DEFENSE
by Thomas E. Krupowicz
ISBN: 1-881690-02-4
9.95

TERK did it again. He wrote another great book!

Finish eating and you can read more of TERK's books!

Oh, TERK's lost his eye glasses again!

CONTENTS	PAGE
1. DEAD MEN DON'T DRINK VODKA	1
2. MAMA, PLEASE DON'T BLOW THAT WHISTLE	13
3. HANS	43
4. THE FORGOTTEN MEMORY	59
5. MISTER HARDLUCK	72
6. THE LAST BUBBLE	79
7. FRATERNALLY YOURS	89
8. SHORT PRAYER FOR A STRANGER	98
9. THE SIZZLING SOUND	115
10. SECRETS OF SILENT LAKE	120

This book is dedicated to my son Tom and daughter-in-law Ruth, my three granddaughters, Spring, Tiffany and Kylie, my daughter Pam and son-in-law Steve and my son Mike and my future daughter-in-law Linda.

DEAD MEN DON'T DRINK VODKA

CHAPTER I

Johnny Casino exited his car, slamming the car door shut behind him. He was mad as hell. The sun had just gone down to let everyone rest for the night. A light snowfall had begun to cover the street and parked cars. Car traffic on the street was heavy. Cars quickly sped passed Johnny with their headlights aglow.

He tucked his crutches into his arm pits before he attacked the challenge of crossing the main boulevard. He slipped, hobbled and dodged the moving cars as he made his way across the wide street.

Becoming the victor of his chosen quest, he stopped walking when he was standing in front of *SHOOTER'S SPORTS BAR AND GRILL*. His stomach still in knots, he was undecided if he really wanted to go into the joint. Balancing himself on his crutches, he looked at his wrist watch. 5:30 p.m. It was still too early to go back home.

Oh what the hell, he thought, I'll just throw down a few brews. He made his way to the entrance door and pulled it open. Making sure that the entrance way was clear, he hobbled into the bar with the help of his crutches.

The lounge's atmosphere was dismal and dimly lit. The bartender, along with five patrons, sat in attendance at the bar. A country and western tune blared out from the juke box's speakers at the far corner of the room.

Johnny made his way to the opposite end of the bar. He dragged a bar stool towards him, wiped off the top of it with his hand, then sat down. He leaned his crutches against the bar - - next to him. His ass was beat and sitting down really felt good. All that he needed now was a beer that was good and cold. He reached into his back pants pocket and took out a black tattered leather wallet. He opened it, removed a $20.00 bill and placed it on top of the bar in front of him.

"Hi, Johnny," said Jack Cags, the bartender.

Johnny frowned, then finally said," Hi, Jack."

"Did the wife throw you out of the house again?" asked the bartender.

"Yea," he paused," it's the old *PMS* time again. If I'm around when it starts, then all hell breaks loose and I seem to catch everything. So, I mind as well sit here then be at home listening to all of her bullshit."

"I see you're still using your crutches," said the bartender. "How long has it been now?" he asked.

"Two months, come this Friday." Johnny Casino continued. "That little son-of-a-bitch that broke my leg with a baseball bat is still in the hospital mending his wounds that I gave him."

"Are those the famous *JAMES BOND* crutches that I've heard about?" asked the bartender, laughing.

"Yep." Johnny Casino picked up one of the crutches and twisted the handle grip. Several small metal blades shot out from the bottom of the crutch. "These are great for walking on icy streets and sidewalks. Keeps me from slipping and falling on my ass."

"Could be a helpful weapon too when needed," said the bartender. "What are you drinking tonight?" he asked.

"Well Jack, I'll tell you. I originally came in for a couple of cold brews, but as long as I'm here visiting with a lot of my old friends..."

The bartender glanced around the bar and saw that no other friends of Johnny's had come in, then interrupted Johnny, "What old friends?" he asked

Johnny smiled and pointed his finger at the wall behind the bartender. "You know my friends. The ones standing over there - - *OLD CROW... JACK DANIEL'S...OLD GRAND DAD...* and the rest of the old crew." Both men laughed

"OK, now what'll you have?" the bartender asked again.

"Aw, what the hell," Johnny hesitated a moment as he viewed the opened bottles of alcohol, "give me a large vodka and grapefruit juice mix. I mind as well enjoy myself. Besides, if I drink too much beer, I build up gas, and all that gas makes me fart."

Both men laughed again. The bartender picked up a clean glass from under the bar, put several ice cubes into it and filled the glass with vodka and grapefruit mix, pouring them together. He speared a maraschino cherry with a small plastic straw, put it into the glass and placed the glass on top of the bar in front of Johnny Casino.

Johnny picked up the glass, looked at the ingredients for a moment, then took a short sip from the glass. He placed the glass down on the bar, lit up a cigarette, took a long drag, then surveyed the people sitting at the opposite end of the bar.

A young woman, approximately 30 years of age, sat alone smoking a cigarette. A half filled glass rested on the bar in front of her. The uniqueness of her facial structure immediately caught Johnny Casino's attention. She looked beautiful - - and she looked *HOT!* Could she be his conquest for tonight?

Her hair was shinny and black in color. It was pulled back tightly and tied into a pony tail in the back of her head. A bright red ribbon held it intact. Her lipstick was a dark shade of red and her cheeks were slightly blushed. She looked in Johnny's direction, giving him a faint, but warming smile.

Aw yes, he thought, she sure is hot looking. A real foxy lady.

"Jack," he called as he waved to the bartender, "see what the ladies drinking. I'd like to buy her a drink. And," he paused, "ask her if she'd like a little company."

The bartender walked over to where the woman was sitting, leaned over and spoke to her, then turned and walked back to where Johnny was sitting. He removed another glass from under the bar and began mixing a drink.

"She likes drinking vodka with a grapefruit mix too," said Jack. He continued, "And she said she'd love some company."

With that, the young woman slid off of her bar stool, picked up her coat off of the other bar stool and walked over to where Johnny was sitting. She sat down on the bar stool next to him.

"Let me have your coat, "he said as he took it from her hands and placed it on top of his crutches.

"Thanks for the drink, "she said coyly, politely starting up the conversation.

"The pleasures all mine, "Johnny replied. "By the way, my name's Johnny Casino," he said, holding out an out stretched hand.

She grasped his hand with hers and said, "Sonja. Sonja Dolby."

"That's a strange sounding first name you have," replied Johnny, "is that some kind of a European name?"

"It is foreign," she replied, smiling. "It's spelled *S-O-N-J-A*, but it's pronounced as *S-A-N-J-A*, the American version." She picked up her glass, toasted him, then took a sip of the drink. She turned and stared at her image in the mirror on the wall in front of her, waiting for him to continue the conversation.

"Ain't seen you in here before," he said. "I come in quite often. I would have noticed you in here before this."

"First time in here for me," she replied. "I usually do my drinking over on Dayton street at the *CASA del SOL* lounge. I thought that I needed a change of atmosphere."

"Glad you did," said Jack, the bartender, "you brighten the place up for us."

CHAPTER II

The front door to the bar opened. A tall, slender built man walked in carrying four boxes in his arms. He walked over to the three men seated at the end of the bar. The three men drank and conversed with each other, unaware of the approaching man.

"Hey guys," greeted the man carrying the four boxes. They all turned around.

"Hi, Jake," was the simultaneous greeting.

"What's in the boxes, Jake?" asked Rondo Sack, the chubbiest of the three men.

Jake Rivers smiled, then placed a box on the bar in front of each man. Each one picked up his box and examined it carefully. They shook the boxes and each one took a guess as to what the rattling sound inside of the boxes could be.

"What the hell is inside of these boxes, Jake?" asked Joey Bell, the second of the men seated at the bar.

Jake Rivers began his tale. "Mac's wife called me at home this morning and asked if I would drop by her house."

"Sure miss old Mac, "interrupted Jose Perez. "We sure had a good time with Mac on our hunting trips."

"He was always the life of the party," said Rondo Sack. "Always had a joke or was playing tricks on someone. There never was a dull moment when Mac was around."

"I can't believe old Mac's been dead a month now," said Joey Bell. He picked up his glass and toasted the sky. "Good hunting, Mac," he said aloud, then took a drink of his beer and couldn't say any more because the words wouldn't come out.

"Jake Rivers continued. "Mac's wife sure hated those hunting trips that we went on. She told me that Mac would rather go hunting with all of us than go on a trip with her."

"You still didn't tell us what's in those boxes, Jake," Jose Perez interrupted him.

"Yea, and what did Mac's widow want to see you about, Jake?" asked Rondo Sack.

"Well, I'll tell you all exactly what she said to me guys," said Jake, pulling up a bar stool and sitting down. But first, he ordered a cold beer and a shot of Jack Daniels from the bartender.

The bartender ran the tap, filling a tall glass with white foam and an amber colored liquid and placed it on the bar in front of Jake. Jake picked up the glass, drank the liquid, then continued his story. "Mac's wife says to me, Jake, here's a present for you and those three other mother-fuckin bums that always went hunting with Mac. You all had a good time while I sat at home on my ass and waited for him to come home when he was ready. And most of the time he was three sheets to the wind when he did come home. Here are four boxes. One for you and one for each of the other three assholes. Tell your friends that the boxes are from me in Mac's memory!"

"You still didn't tell us what's in the boxes, Jake?" interrupted Joey Bell.

"I'm getting to that. Be patient, "said Jake. He took another sip from his glass of beer, then continued speaking. "Mac's wife had Mac's body cremated. After the undertaker gave her the urn with his ashes in it, she went to a gun shop. She had the shop owner take Mac's ashes and mix it with lead pellets. Then he poured the mixture into 12 gauge shotgun shells. She told me that as long as we were so fond of each other, that we should use these shells the next time we go hunting and blow Mac's ass all over the forest and cow pasture that we hunt in. She also said that she hoped the ashes covered the ground and that the cows would continue covering the ashes. I'm telling you guys, I've never seen a woman so bitter at a man."

Joey Bell laughed, then said, "Well," as he picked up his box, "Mac, old buddy, we're going hunting again this week end."

The four men laughed loudly and then drank heavily.

CHAPTER III

Johnny Casino wasn't paying any attention to the men at the other end of the bar. He was busy scoring points with his latest conquest - - Sonja. He moved closer to her. They stared into each others eyes and said nothing. Johnny moved closer and kissed her lips gently. He played with her soft, moist tongue. Her response was to gently nip the tip of his tongue with her front teeth.

"Hey Johnny," said the bartender, "walk softly but carry a big...."

"Yea, yea, I know," Johnny interrupted, "stick. You're always quoting something for me to live by. There hasn't been a time when I left this place that you didn't give me one of your famous quotes."

Sonja gulped down half of her drink.

Boy, she must really be anxious, thought Johnny. Got to play this cool. Can't blow it now. "Sonja, are you a lady of the night?" he asked.

"I'm a lady of both daylight and moonlight, "she replied unconcerningly. "Why?" she asked.

Johnny Casino remained silent, thinking to himself, because I don't want to have to pay for something that I can get for nothing. That's why. He smiled at her and still remained silent.

Sonja slipped off of the bar stool and picked up her purse off of the bar.

"Where are you going?" Johnny asked.

"Ladies room," she replied, "to powder my nose and take care of a few other things." She walked in the direction of the rest rooms.

"Packin' tonight, Johnny?" asked the bartender.

"No, Jack. You know that when I'm doin some serious drinking, I always leave my piece at home. I don't like to carry my service revolver with me. I still can't remember where I put my other gun the last time I was in here. Boy, you should see the paper work I had to fill out for the department. The captain was mad as hell. Made me walk a post as punishment for a solid month."

"How many years have you got on the department now, Johnny?" asked the bartender.

"Too many to suit me. It won't be long before I'm throwing in the star and taking my pension."

The front door to the bar opened. Three men walked in. They took off their hats, shook them and wiped the snow off of the top of their shoulders. The snow fall outside had intensified. One of the three men stomped both of his feet on the floor, trying to shake the snow off of his shoes.

"Evenin gents," said the bartender, "care to sit at the bar or at a table?" he asked.

One of the men made a gesture with his hand towards a table at the far end of the room, away from everyone, next to the jukebox. The three men walked over to the table, removed their coats, then sat down.

"Could you turn this goddamn thing off?" remarked one of the men. "We'd like to do a little talking."

"Sure," Jack replied as he reached under the bar and flicked a switch with his finger. The jukebox went dark and the music stopped playing.

"Thank you," said the third man of the group. "Bring us all a cold round of beer." The three men leaned forward and began to whisper to each other.

CHAPTER IV

Sonja came out of the restroom and went back to her seat at the bar.

"Feel any better? Everything come out OK?" asked Johnny Casino, smiling.

"Well," she answered, "the pressure's off and the pole can rise." She picked up her glass and finished the rest of her drink. "Another, please," she asked.

Huh? Thought Johnny. This broad must be nuts. She's been quoting some weird shit to me tonight.

Jack Cags removed the metal caps off of three bottles of beer and placed them on a tray along with three empty glasses. He picked up the tray and walked over to the table where the three men were sitting. "That'll be six bucks gents," he said.

One of the men took a $10.00 bill out of his pocket and gave it to Jack. He walked back behind the bar, made change and came back to the table, dropping four single dollar bills in the middle of it. "Thanks," said Jack. "If anyone else wants anything more, just yell out."

The next half hour passed routinely. The bartender washed, wiped and cleaned glasses. Johnny Casino was building up points with Sonja and the four hunters kept drinking and laughing.

The bartender turned on the television to listen to the 7:00 p.m. news.

"Hey, shut that goddamn thing off," shouted one of the men from the table.

"Just take it easy pal," replied the bartender, "we want to listen to the news of the day."

"Yea," interrupted Johnny Casino, "and we want to hear the weather report too." The bartender continued. "I'll turn the TV off when the news is over. The sound will be quiet enough so you can still carry on your conversation."

Luke, the tallest and biggest built of the three men, slid his chair back from the table and stood up. His face flushed. Cal, who was sitting to Luke's right, grabbed hold of his friend's arm.

"Just sit down Luke and shut up," he commanded. "You'll blow this whole fuckin deal with that short temper of yours."

Aaron, the third member of the group, nodded his head in approval at Cal's last statement.

"Assholes!" mumbled the bartender under his breath as he began watching and listening to the news commentator. He slowly dried a wet glass.

Cal leaned forward. This conversation was only for the ears of the group. "Luke, that damn temper of yours is going to screw us up. Just cool it and do what I tell you to do."

"OK, Cal, whatever you say," answered Luke, apologetically.

"Hey, Cal," Aaron interrupted, "you came down to Feyetville to get us to help you with this caper of yours. I like being back home in South Carolina where it's warm. You can keep this cold Chicago weather." Aaron lit up a cigarette. He continued. "Now, just tell us the whole story of why you brought us here to Chicago."

"Look guys," Cal began. "It's a sweet deal and it's going to bring us a lot of money... if we handle it in the right way. We can't afford any screw-ups in any way or form. Listen to me carefully. I've been hired by a woman to kill her husband."

"What! Are you nuts?" shouted Aaron. "You want us to...."

"Keep your god-damn voice down," said Cal, angrily. He continued. "For some reason, bad blood had developed between the woman and her husband. She gave me a hint that he's possibly playing around with another woman. But, get this. The guy's heavily insured. She gave me three grand and said she'd pay me seventeen grand more when the job was finished. That's twenty big ones for us to split up."

"Yea," Luke interrupted again, "and where are we supposed to hit this guy?" he asked.

"Right across the street, at the corner of the block." said Cal. " He supposedly has a dinner date at the restaurant for 8:00 p.m. We'll stay here awhile and have a few brews while we wait and give him time enough to have his last meal. We'll hit him when he leaves the restaurant."

"What's our jobs?" asked Aaron.

"Yea, and who does the hitting?" asked Luke, excited by the whole idea.

"Shut up and let me go on," said Cal. "Just listen carefully. Where did you park your car?"

Luke pointed in the opposite direction of the restaurant. "We parked the pick-up truck over there," he said.

"*Jesus H. Christ*," exclaimed Cal, "did you bring that broken down old pick-up truck of yours?"

"We didn't have time to steal a car and meet with you on time."

"Where's your car, Cal?" asked Luke.

"I took a cab here. I was counting on you guys for the getaway car. OK," he paused, "here's what we do. After we make the hit, Aaron will do the driving. I'll get into the passenger seat and Luke," he paused again, "you'll have to jump in the back of the pick-up truck. It'll be cold and wet, but its gonna have to do till we get away from the neighborhood."

"When do we get our money, Cal?" asked Luke. "I sure would like to hold my seven grand in my own hands."

"Seven Grand," exclaimed Cal, "you're not getting that much, Luke. I'm taking ten grand for my share and you two are splitting up the other ten grand. I got us the job and I'm making the money pick up."

"Then you can do the shooting too," said Aaron.

"Yea," Luke agreed.

"OK ... OK," said Cal, holding both of his hands up in the air. "I'll do the shooting and that's why I'm taking 50% of the payoff!"

The bartender saw Cal's hands waving in the air. "Another round, guys?" he yelled.

The bartender's suggestion startled Cal. "Yea," he immediately replied. "Bring us all another round of drinks."

CHAPTER V

Jake Rivers and Jose Perez broke up the hunters 4--some by going home at 7:55 p.m. The bartender had turned the TV off and was filling up the cooler with bottles of warm beer.

Cal held the front door slightly ajar, watching for a car to pull up with the license number that his client had given him. The two hunters excused themselves as they squeezed passed Cal. Johnny Casino continued to fondle Sonja's anatomy.

At exactly 8:05 p.m., a black Cadallic pulled up in front of the corner restaurant. It bore the license plate number that Cal was given - - 666.

That's it, thought Cal. They're here. He watched the valet open the car door for the woman passenger, then run around to the other side of the car. He entered the car, then drove away.

The male companion put the parking receipt into his coat pocket and escorted the young woman into the restaurant.

Cal quickly walked back to the table where his two friends were sitting. He leaned towards them. "They're here," he whispered, excited. He sat down. "OK," he continued, "this is what we're going to do. At 9:00 p.m. we'll all go outside. Aaron will turn the truck around, facing towards the restaurant and park as close as he can get to the restaurant's doorway. I'll wait in the truck with him. Luke, you'll be in the doorway of the building directly across from the restaurant. When they come out, I'll get out of the truck, make the hit and we'll make our getaway. Luke, you have to make sure he's not moving after I make the hit. If he is, put both barrels of your shotgun into his head. Don't hesitate... just do it! We'll jump into the truck when we finish, and Aaron will drive away. That's it. That's the whole plan. Any one got any suggestions to make?" he asked.

"What about the broad that's with the guy?" asked Aaron.

"If she's smart, she'll duck and get out of the way when she spots me coming and things start to happen. If she doesn't move, then it's just too bad for her!"

CHAPTER VI

At 8:30 p.m. Cal finished the rest of his beer. "Time we got started," he said.

"I've got to take a piss, Cal, " said Luke, crossing his legs tightly. "All that beer we drank is starting to leak out of my bladder."

"Go ahead, we'll wait for you," said Aaron as he slipped on his outer coat.

Sonja threw her head back and laughed loudly at the dirty joke that Johnny Casino had just told to her.

As Luke walked passed her, on his way to the washroom, he felt a strong urge to give a quick yank on Sonja's pony tail. Since grade school, that always had been one of his worst habits, yanking on pony tails.

Luke took hold of Sonja's hair with his hand and gave a quick tug. A look of surprise appeared on everyone's face. Luke stopped walking and stood motionless, holding a black hair piece in his left hand.

"I'll be damned," said the bartender. "*SHE'S A HE!*"

Johnny Casino was speechless. He was stunned. What was sitting next to him. He made a fist with his hand and swung at Sonja. She ducked. He missed her. "Just what the hell is your real name?" he screamed.

"Arthur," replied the impersonator.

"*I'll kill ya*," Johnny screamed as he swung again - - missed -- fell off of the bar stool ... bouncing his ass on the floor.

Luke ran back to the table where his friends sat. They watched in amazement. Luke's bladder didn't hurt anymore. The front of his pants was wet. He yanked his outer coat off of his chair. His double barreled, sawed-off shotgun fell out of the jacket and hit the floor. He picked up his weapon and shouted, "*Don't no one move. Everyone stand still where you're at.*"

The female impersonator, almost reaching the front door, stopped and didn't take another step.

Johnny Casino scrambled over the fallen bar stool, trying to pick himself up. The bartender dropped the glass he was wiping. The two hunters stared at Luke and said nothing.

"*SHIT*," screamed Cal.

"This kind of screws up the plan, doesn't it Cal?" said Aaron.

"You bet your ass it does," he barked. He looked at Luke. "*Dumb, clumsy asshole*," he shouted.

Luke looked surprised by Cal's sudden outburst. He thought he had handled the situation properly. Why was Cal mad at him?

Cal pulled a gun out of his pant's waistband. "Everyone move over by the jukebox," he ordered. "Don't talk. Just quickly move your asses. Aaron, check them over for weapons. Luke, cover them while Aaron does the searching," he ordered. Aaron and Luke did as they were instructed.

Cal opened the front door and looked towards the restaurant. The person he was supposed to kill was standing at the curb with his lady friend, waiting for his car.

"Holy shit," he blurted out as he looked towards his cohorts. "The guy is standing at the curb waiting for his car. We've got to move fast. Luke, you stay here and watch those people. Keep them quiet. Have them sit or lay on the floor. Aaron, go stand in the doorway across the street...hidden from view. I'm gonna walk over to the restaurant, cross the street and hit him where he stands. If for some reason he gets past me, you can come out of the doorway and finish the job. Hurry, we don't have much time."

Johnny Casino picked up his crutches and hobbled over to the jukebox. He dropped his crutches and sat down on the floor. The bartender and the rest of the patrons gathered in front of the jukebox. Luke pointed his shotgun directly at them. "Everyone sit down and shut up," he ordered. They all complied. The bartender sat between Johnny and the female impersonator. Johnny Casino leaned forward and looked at the impersonator.

"I'm gonna break your fuckin neck when this is all over," he said, loud enough for everyone to hear him.

Luke pulled back the hammers on his shotgun. "I told everyone to shut-up," he repeated. He pointed the shotgun at Johnny Casino.

"Hey, just take it easy, pal," said the bartender. "We'll all be as quiet as church mice."

Cal and Aaron left the lounge. Aaron ran across the street and hid in the dark shadows of the doorway -- ready and waiting. Cal trotted down the sidewalk, crushing the new fallen snow under each step that he took. His hand tightly clutched the revolver that he concealed in his outer coat pocket. He carefully watched his target as he began the final stage of his stalking game.

Cal removed the revolver from his coat pocket as he began to cross the street in front of his intended target. The passing cars swerved so as not to hit him and blew their horns in retaliation for their forceful change of direction. The loud noise caught the target's attention. He saw Cal coming towards him with a crazed look in his eyes. Cal brought up his revolver to eye level and pulled the trigger twice. As he fired, he lost his footing on a patch of ice on the street. The first bullet struck the large plate glass window of the restaurant, shattering it into a thousand pieces. The second bullet struck the neon sign hanging above the entrance to the restaurant.

The intended target fell to his knees on the sidewalk and hid behind a metal mail box for protection. People waiting for taxicabs scattered in all different directions for protection.

The female escort with the target, pulled a 9mm automatic pistol from her purse. She fell to one knee, used a street light pole for protection, aimed her automatic and pulled the trigger repeatedly. A rally of gun shots rang out. First three shots - - than two more - - again two - - finally three more.

Silence prevailed for a long moment, then shots rang out in the street again - - first two - - followed by three more.

Cal lay dead in the middle of the snow covered street. Aaron staggered and fell dead in the middle of the sidewalk.

Luke began to perspire. He didn't know what to do. All those gun shots and car crash noises coming from the street outside made him extremely nervous. He wanted to vomit and just get away from this crazy situation.

Should he stay? Should he run away? What should he do with the hostages? Shoot them? Forget about them? Cal never told him really what to do with them. Why the hell wasn't Cal and Aaron coming back into the lounge to get him?

Luke kept glancing between the front door and his hostages, moving the shotgun back and forth as he shifted his weight on his feet. The hammers on the shotgun were still in the cocked position... ready to fire.

Got to make my move the next time he turns his head, thought Johnny Casino. It's now or never. He's getting too fidgety to suit me.

The front door of the lounge opened. A stranger to everyone walked in. Luke turned his head and barrel of the shotgun to see who the man was. Johnny Casino picked up one of his crutches and twisted the hand grip. The small sharp blades sprang out from the bottom of the crutch. He leaped forward, driving the sharp blades into Luke's right knee cap.

Luke screamed in pain, turning the barrel of the shotgun towards the hostages. At the same time that Johnny took action - - so did the bartender. He leaped forward too, grabbing hold of the shotgun's barrel and pointed it towards the ceiling.

Luke fell backwards, his leg reeking with pain as his pants turned a crimson color. Luke hit the floor. His fingers automatically pulled the triggers of both barrels on the shotgun. Two loud explosions deafened everyone. A bright flash -- a cloud of blue smoke -- a large chunk of ceiling plaster surrounding a large light fixture crashed to the floor. Johnny Casino yanked the shotgun from Luke's grasp and hit him across the forehead with the butt of it. A deep red gash appeared on Luke's forehead. He didn't move.

CHAPTER VII

By 11:30 p.m., everything was over. The police cars and ambulances that had been summoned, had removed the dead and the injured. The hunters had gone home. Sonja had split as soon as he could leave. He didn't want Johnny Casino getting a hold of him after he had seen what he had done to Luke with the shotgun butt.

The lounge was peaceful once again. Johnny and the bartender sat at the bar - - talking.

"Tell me, Johnny," said the bartender, "what the hell happened out there on the street? What was all the shooting? I know that you got the whole low down from your district friends."

Johnny smiled, but first took a sip of his vodka and grapefruit mixed drink before he answered his friend. "Here's the story that I got, Jack. When he came to, the officers questioned the guy that was holding us hostage. His name was Luke. He said that they had been hired to kill a man that was eating dinner at the corner restaurant. The intended victim's wife had hired them. How do you like those apples?"

"Well, I guess a wife likes a change of pace once in awhile," said the bartender - - laughing as he spoke.

Johnny Casino continued. "Yea...well, unbeknown to them, the woman that was having dinner with the intended target was actually his own personal bodyguard. The dinner party was really a business meeting that was held between the target and some government officials. The woman was just a decoy. She's really an undercover police officer with the Intelligence Unit assigned to protect his life. Government secrets, as well as narcotics, were being sent across the United States by use of his products and trucks. He had a good idea who it was and they were comprising a plan to break up the organization.

"The intended target's life was threatened several times. He asked the police for protection and the lady cop was assigned to him. He didn't want to tell his wife about the threats so as not to worry her. I guess she thought that he was cheating on her and she didn't want to lose her nest egg. But, she wanted revenge," Johnny paused. "Those two yokels sure got one hell-of-a surprise when they tried to hit him."

The bartender scratched the back of his head, then replied, "I'll be damned. That's one hell-of-a- story and to think that it all happened here in my place of business."

"Yea... well... you're gonna have to watch who you let in here from now on," said Johnny after he took another long swallow of his drink.

"You know Johnny, it took a lot of guts to go after that guy with that crutch of yours. Suppose he would have stepped back and you missed his leg?" asked Jack Cags.

"You, I and the others would probably be dead, but you took care of that when you pushed the shotgun barrel towards the ceiling."

"And when I think about it now," said the bartender, "it was a dumb move and it sure scared the hell out of me."

"Well, anyway, I'm glad that you did, Jack. It saved all of our lives." Johnny Casino slid off of his bar stool and put a crutch under each arm. "Well," he continued, "I think I'll go home and smooch with the wife for awhile. Too much action around here for me tonight."

"Hey, Johnny," said the bartender, "just one more thing. You were going pretty hot and heavy with that girlfriend of yours tonight. What was his name again? Oh yes, Sonja."

"No... Arthur... but let's just forget all about that," remarked Johnny as he reached the front door of the lounge. He opened the door, then stopped. Turning around, he looked at his friend and asked, "None of your famous proverbs for me tonight before I leave, Jack?"

The bartender hesitated a moment, then smiled and said, "Yea, I got one for you, Johnny. Just remember one thing... *DEAD MEN DON'T DRINK VODKA!*"

MAMA, PLEASE DON'T BLOW THAT

WHISTLE

The clock radio came to life at exactly 6:30 a.m., blaring out music produced by one of the local rock and roll stations. Verna Gateman walked sluggishly into her dining room carrying a silver serving tray. A lock of her brown and grayish hair swayed from side to side in front of her eyes as she passed under the archway separating the kitchen and dining room. A container of hot coffee and four China coffee cups rattled on the tray as she walked. She quickly set the tray down on top of the dining room table and rushed back into the kitchen to turn the radio off.

"Such music I don't need so early in the morning," she mumbled aloud to herself. She rebuttoned some of the buttons on the front of the tattered housecoat that she wore. Picking up a fist full of silverware and four plates, she walked back into the dining room.

Verna Gateman hummed a lively Jewish folk tune while she finished setting the highly polished dining room table for the breakfast meal. Glancing on the clock hanging on the living room wall, she turned and walked to her daughter's bedroom door. She knocked loudly on the door while speaking.

"*Sherry... wake up*," she shouted, continuing to knock on the closed door. "Are you awake yet?" she asked. "If not, then wake up now. Breakfast is ready."

"Oh, have a little mercy ma. Stop the pounding. I'm awake," a woman's voice shouted from inside the bedroom.

Verna Gateman smiled. She continued to hum her favorite folk tune as she walked to the opposite side of the dining room.

"*Sam*," she shouted into the darkened hallway, "get up or you'll be late for work." The bathroom door suddenly swung open. Sam Gateman stuck his soap lathered face out into the hallway. "*I'm up, Verna*," he shouted. "*For Christ sake... I'm up.*"

"Is Dexter in there with you?" she asked, rebuttoning her house coat again.

"Verna, this is only a one person bathroom and I'm the only one who's using it now. Knock on your son's door and shock him back into this world with that beautiful, vibrant voice of yours. The poor soul probably didn't get in till 4 a.m. this morning."

"Sam, don't be picking on the boy all the time," Verna continued, "he's only lining up clients for his future law practice."

"Clients...*Ha!*" Sam shouted. "At the rate he's going, he's going to be the cause of 50 percent of the divorce cases coming up next year." Sam Gateman pushed back the curly black hair from his eyes, then slammed the bathroom door shut. He continued shaving in privacy.

Verna Gateman called out her son's name while she pounded on his bedroom door. "*Dexter... Dexter dear. Are you awake yet?*" she asked loudly.

A confused voice from behind the door replied, "Huh? What? Yea. Huh-huh."

Verna continued, "Dexter dear, wake up. This is your mother speaking to you."

This time, no response came from inside the bedroom. The bathroom door suddenly swung open. Sam Gateman stormed over to where his wife was standing. Making a tight fist with his right hand, he pounded on his son's bedroom door, shouting, "*Dexter, you crazy fool, get out of there right now. Her husband is coming in the front door.*"

Sam Gateman moved his 6 foot 3 inch muscular frame back into the bathroom, closing the door behind him. Dexter's bedroom door suddenly swung open. Dexter Gateman, his eyes half open, ran out into the hallway carrying his pants, shirt and shoes in his arms.

"Breakfast is ready Dexter dear. Get dressed," said Verna, patting her son on his cheek with her hand. Smiling and humming, she returned to the dining room - - turned - - then headed for the kitchen.

CHAPTER II

At 6:50 a.m., everyone was sitting at the dining room table dressed in their pajamas and robes.

"Eat more of your breakfast," insisted Verna.

"I've had enough to eat, mama," replied Sherry, "I'm on a diet and I've got to watch my waist line."

"Again, you're on a diet," Verna remarked sarcastically. "First you played with the color of your hair... from brown to red... then to white. Now you play with your waist line. Better you should watch the boys, then find yourself a husband and he can watch your waist line for you. Sherry," Verna paused, "here you are, 21 years old, pretty and you're not even engaged. Mark my words young lady, you'll wind up to be an old spinster with no family of your own."

"Mama, let's not go over that old boring subject again," Sherry pleaded. "I've told you time and time again, I'm having to much fun right now to think about getting a husband. A girl is just starting to know herself and find out what life's all about when she reaches my age. There's plenty of time for marriage, mama."

"Huh. A lot you know young lady," Verna interrupted her daughter. "I should already be a grandmother. A bouncing happy grandchild sitting on my lap."

"Leave the girl be, Verna," interrupted Sam Gateman, "she'll get married when she's good and ready." He buttered another piece of raisin toast, then took a big bite out of it.

"Never you mind, Sam, "protested Verna, getting excited as she spoke. She pointed her index finger at he son, shaking it from side to side. "It's your son sitting over there that you should be worried about. At the pace he's going he will be the main attraction in every divorce case held in the courts for the next two years."

Dexter Gateman ignored the conversation being discussed at the table and just sipped hot coffee from his cup.

"By the way young man," said Sam Gateman as he looked directly at his son, "you've been out of the army for six months. When are you going to find yourself a job?"

"I'm recovering from the perils of war, pa," Dexter answered his father. He picked up a piece of toast. "It takes a long time to readjust to the civilian ways of living again." He buttered the toast.

"And just how do you account for the way you've been fooling around with all those women?" asked his father.

"They're just the first step back to rehabilitation, pa," answered Dexter, smiling. "Why,"he paused a moment,"in another six months everything should be back to normal for me."

"Six months!" shouted Sam Gateman, almost choking on a piece of toast. "You mean to tell me that you don't plan on going back to work for another six months?"

"Drink your coffee, Sam," said Verna, pouring a fresh cup of the hot liquid for her husband. "You'll be late for your roll call again."

Sam Gateman stood up, threw his napkin on the table and started to leave the dining room. He stopped and turned towards his wife. "Did you sew the button on my police pants, Verna?" he asked.

"Yes Sam, I did," she answered as she rebuttoned the bottom of her house coat again. "Your pants are hanging up in your closet." Sam Gateman left the room.

"Children," whispered Verna, "you shouldn't annoy your father so early in the morning. He has to many thoughts going through his mind."

Sam Gateman came back into the dining room carrying a pair of dark blue pants in his hand. "Verna," he said disgustedly, "are these the pants that you fixed for me?" he asked.

"Why yes, Sam," she replied, "what's wrong with them?"

"Verna," Sam continued, "what did I ask you to do with these pants?"

"You told me I should sew a button on them. So I did. So what's the big problem that's upsetting you?" Verna began getting excited again.

"*Look... Verna ... Look!*" Sam shouted, holding the pants out in front of him for everyone to see. "You sewed the button on the pants all right, but you sewed the button and both pieces of material together. How in the hell am I suppose to put these pants on, Verna? You want I should shimmy into them like you put on your girdle?" he asked.

"Don't be silly, Sam," answered Verna unconcerningly, "just leave them on the couch and I'll fix them for you again later on in the day."

"Forget it, Verna," Sam snapped. "I'll take them to the tailor shop. Morris will fix them for me. Verna," he paused with concern," I don't know what's gotten into you lately. Everything that you attempt to do is done wrong. Maybe you should go and see Doctor Melton. He may have some memory retaining pills for people who are getting on in their years." Sam turned and left the room. He remained in his bedroom a few minutes, finished dressing, then left the apartment, slamming the front door shut behind him.

Everyone sat speechless at the table. Sherry stood up and walked over to her mother. She placed her hand on Verna's shoulder. "Don't worry, ma," she said softly, "dad's just a little upset right now. It's like you said before, he's got a lot on his mind."

"No, Sherry," replied Verna, sighing, "your papa is right. Every time I try to do something right, something goes wrong. These past few weeks have been terrible for me. Like the time I wanted to clean Sam's favorite pipe. I scrubbed the pipe with kitchen cleanser. I wanted the inside of the pipe to dry out completely, so I put the pipe in the clothes dryer. I set the controls on the lowest heat setting. I never dreamed that the pipe would melt. It took your father six hours to scrape the melted plastic off of the tumbling drum," Verna continued, almost in tears as she spoke. "And then there was the time I was going to wash your father's pants and colored sport shirts. When I poured some bleach into the washing machine, I could have sworn that the tub was full of water. Those clothes were streaked so badly that your father had to buy himself a new wardrobe. No Sherry, your father is right. Something is definitely wrong with me and I don't know exactly what it is. Yes, I'll have to make an appointment to see Doctor Melton."

"If you insist, ma," replied Sherry, kissing he mother softly on her cheek. "Do what you think is best for you. But for now, I'm running late for school and I have to finish dressing."

Dexter Gateman looked at his wrist watch, gulped down the rest of his coffee and stood up. "I didn't realize it was so late. I have an early appointment downtown this morning."

Verna sipped her hot coffee slowly, then looked up at her son. "Sit down, Dexter," she said softly, "I want you and I should have a nice little talk together." She looked at her daughter. "And you too, Sherry. When you come home from school this afternoon, we're going to have a nice little talk too."

"Anything you say, ma," said Sherry as she rushed into her bedroom.

Dexter reluctantly sat back down in his chair just as his mother had requested. Sherry hurried out of her bedroom, kissed her mother on the cheek and left the apartment. Dexter poured himself another cup of hot coffee. He knew just what his mother was going to say. They had discussed this subject many times before.

"Dexter," Verna began, "you know that what your father says is right. Registration for school ends next month. You've been doing nothing about your future. And since you can't make up your own mind," she hesitated a moment, "someone has to make up your mind for you. By the end of this month, I want you should either be working or going to school. That is my mind... I've made it up!"

"Ma, that phrase goes like this," he said smiling, "I've made up my mind and that's that."

"Stop correcting your mother and do what I tell you to do," she snapped angrily.

"OK, ma. OK," he replied, still smiling, "I'll make up my mind by the end of next week. I promise. Come the end of the month, I'll either be working or going to school. But now, I really must hurry. I do have that important meeting this morning and if I don't hurry I'll be late for it." He stood up, kissed his mother on her cheek and went into his bedroom to finish dressing.

Verna poured herself another cup of coffee. Adding a few drops of cream, she slowly stirred the dark brown mixture until it turned a light tan in color. She picked up the morning paper and turned to the section dedicated to women readers.

She had finished reading a few paragraphs when her son walked out of his bedroom. Dressed in a white shirt, tan colored tie and dark brown suit, he again approached his mother and kissed her gently on her cheek. "I'm leaving now, ma. Have a good day." He left the apartment.

Verna smiled, hesitated a moment, then went back to reading the newspaper.

CHAPTER III

A half hour went by. Verna set the newspaper down and turned on the television set. It was time for her favorite soap opera's - - three hours of heavy heartbreaking drama. Resting herself in her favorite, comfortable winged-back chair, she prepared herself for a morning of television fantasy.

The front doorbell startled her. Its loud tones echoed throughout the apartment.

"*Who is it?*" she asked, shouting.

"It's me. Your favorite neighbor," the reply came back. "It's Sarah ... Sarah Betz."

"Just a moment, Sarah." Verna stood up, walked to the front door and struggled with the safety latch. Got to have this fixed one of these days, she thought to herself.

Sarah Betz waited impatiently in the hallway. She was dressed in an old flannel robe, no make-up on her face, fake fur slippers and her head was covered with hair curlers. "Are you alone. Verna?" she asked, hoping that no one was around to see what see looked like.

"Yes, I'm alone," answered Verna as she finally got the door to open.

"Have you any hot coffee left, Verna? My coffee pot stopped working this morning. If I don't get a cup of coffee soon I think I'll go out of my mind."

"There's half a pot full left, Sarah. Come on in. We can both have a cup while we chat and watch television."

Sarah Betz entered the apartment. Her slippers made a loud plopping sound when she walked. She approached the couch and sat down. "I'm glad you're watching my favorite program, Verna," she remarked, "my television set went on the frizz last week."

Verna lifted the coffee pot off of the table and carefully poured two cups full of coffee. "Do you want cream and sugar?" she asked her friend.

"Just a little cream, Verna. I'm on a diet this week." Sarah Betz relocated herself on the couch, searching for the best and most comfortable spot to sit.

"Everyone's on a diet these days," said Verna, snickering as she poured the cream into the coffee cup and secretly put a teaspoon of sugar into her friend's cup of coffee.

"Do you mind if I borrow one of your cigarettes, Verna?" asked Sarah. "I ran out last night and haven't had time to go out and get some this morning."

"Help yourself, Sarah." Verna walked over to the couch and set the cups down on the coffee table. She sat herself down next to her friend. "Sarah," she began, "I've got a problem and I'm very concerned about it. There's something wrong with me and I don't know just what is happening to me."

Sarah picked up her cup, sipped the coffee, then set the cup down. She lit another cigarette. "You can confide in me, Verna. Tell me what's really troubling you. Are you and Sam having marriage problems?" she asked.

"No, it's nothing like that!" Verna snapped back. Sarah continued speaking, ignoring her friend's last remark. "I know, you're having an affair with our mailman and you're pregnant, right?"

"Sarah, stop talking foolishly," said Verna, angry at her friends last suggestion. "That type of situation was on a soap opera that was on last week. I'm fifty-four years old. What would I be doing having an affair at my age?" she asked bashfully.

"You'd be having a hell of a lot of fun and not worrying about what's wrong with you," replied her friend. She took another sip of her coffee.

"Be serious, Sarah," Verna pleaded, "try and help me."

Sarah leaned against the back of the couch and looked directly at her friend. "All right, Verna," she said, "do you want to know what I think your problem is?" she asked.

"Yes. What?" pleaded Verna, becoming really concerned.

"You're going through a change of life! Female problems girl! That's all my dear," answered her friend.

"*A change of life...ha!*" shouted Verna, throwing both hands up into the air.

"You can *ha-ha* all you want, Verna, but the fact still remains that you're probably going through a drastic change." Her friend continued as Verna listened attentively. "Just answer a few questions for me. Are you irritable all of the time? Do your nerves feel as if they were going to pop through your skin? Do you snap at Sam and the children for the least little thing they do that irritates you? Are you forgetful? Do you get hot and cold flashes?"

Verna remained silent as she thought to herself. All the answers to her friend's questions were - - *yes*.

"The answer is *yes* to all of your questions, Sarah," she finally confessed aloud, surprised at her friend hitting the nail right on the head. "But how could you know about all of these things?" she asked as she rebuttoned her house coat again.

Sarah took hold of her friend's hand and squeezed it firmly. "Verna," she began, a tone of friendship and reassurance in her voice, "I know all about those problems. Last month I completed my correspondence courses on physiology and psychology. One of the chapters dealt with just what we're talking about right now. Have a little faith in me Verna. I'm positive that I can help you."

"I was going to call Doctor Melton this morning," interrupted Verna, "and make an appointment to see him.'

"*Forget about the doctor*," Sarah shouted angrily. "All he'll do is take your money and tell you the same thing that I'm going to tell you right now."

Verna Gateman sat still and remained silent. She looked inside of her coffee cup. It was empty. She stood, picked up both coffee cups and walked over to the dining room table. Picking up the coffee pot, she filled both cups with the hot liquid. Sarah lit up another cigarette.

Verna placed the two coffee cups down on the cocktail table, walked over to the television set and turned it off. She went back to the couch and sat down. "All right Sarah, I'll listen to what you have to say. Just help me. What do we have to do first?" she asked. Verna was ready to do whatever her friend suggested.

Sarah put out her cigarette. She picked up her coffee cup and slowly sipped the hot liquid. "Verna," she began, "we have to study your problem from every angle. We have to figure out a plan of strategy. Each person is special in their own little way, each with a different problem and each needing a different solution for that problem. Now, in your case, I would say that you have to think things out before you open your mouth to speak. If a problem arises, think of a way that you can attack that problem and come up the winner of the situation. If something has been bothering you, attack that problem and make the results turn out the way you want them to."

Sarah paused a moment, then picked up the pack of cigarettes off of the cocktail table. "You're out of cigarettes, Verna. Have you another pack?" she asked.

"Yes, Sarah, I have. I'll get them for you. "Verna walked into the kitchen and returned with a fresh pack of cigarettes. She handed them to her friend. Sarah ripped off the cellophane seal, took out a cigarette, lit it, then continued with her diagnosis.

"As I see it, Verna, we have to find a way to take care of that delicate temper of yours. What you need is an object that will be your pillar of strength. Whenever you feel yourself getting ready to blow your top, you must grab hold of this object, squeeze it tightly and let your anger and frustration slowly transfer from your body into the object that you are holding. I guarantee you that within minutes you'll be feeling like your old self again."

Sarah took a long drag from her cigarette and let the bluish cloud of smoke rise towards the ceiling. She continued speaking. "Now follow my instructions carefully, Verna. Close your eyes and squeeze them tight so that all you can see is total darkness. Erase every thought from your mind. Leave your mind a complete blank. Are you following my instructions, Verna?" she asked.

"Yes Sarah, my mind is a complete blank." Sarah continued. "Verna, think of a light blue sky with soft white clouds passing overhead."

Verna visualized her friend's instructions.

"When I count to three, Verna, I want you to open your eyes. The first object that you will see will be the object that will be your pillar of strength. Sarah began. " One... two... three!"

Verna Gateman opened her eyes.

"What was the first object that you saw, Verna?" asked her friend.

Verna leaned towards the cocktail table and picked up her husband's black, bakelite police whistle.

"*That's it! That's it Verna*!" Sarah shouted excitedly. "That whistle will be your pillar of strength. Every time you get angry or disturbed about something, blow that whistle till you feel relieved. Try it Verna. Try it now!"

Verna Gateman puckered her lips, took a deep breath and blew into the whistle. A shrilling shriek echoed through the apartment. Sarah quickly covered both her ears with her hands, trying to keep out the loud piercing sound. Verna continued blowing the whistle.

"Enough Verna...Please! That's enough, "Sarah pleaded. Verna finally stopped.

"You've got the idea, Verna. Now follow my instructions and I'm positive that we can solve that problem of yours. Get yourself a small chain and let the whistle hang around your neck. In that way, it will always be handy whenever you need it."

Verna left her friend sitting on the couch and went into her bedroom. She rummaged through her jewelry box. After a few minutes, she returned to the living room carrying a small chain from an old necklace that she had found. She slid the chain through the small metal ring at the end of the whistle, then fastened the chain and placed it around her neck.

"How does it look, Sarah?" she inquired.

"It looks very nice on you, Verna," answered her friend. "You can wear it when Sam takes you out dining and dancing. And also, besides being your pillar of strength, that whistle will give you some protection against muggers and purse snatchers."

Verna smiled and rebuttoned her housecoat again. Sarah picked up the pack of cigarettes off of the cocktail table and put them into her pocket. She patted her friend's hand. "Well, Verna," she said, "I really must be going. I have a luncheon date with a few of the girls today. I'll get back to you in a few days to see just how things are working out with the whistle."

Both women stood, then walked to the front door. Verna opened the door. They bid each other good-bye and before Sarah finished walking through the doorway, Verna closed the door. The sound of tearing material followed the scream of a frantic woman out in the hallway. Verna quickly opened the door. Her friend's robe lay on the floor - - half of it in the hallway and the other half in Verna's apartment. Verna stuck her head out into the hallway just in time to see her friend running to her apartment, clad in only a white bra and a pair of black underpants.

Tears fell freely from the milkman's eyes, as he laughed hysterically, while trying to salvage some of the milk bottles that he had just dropped on the floor.

Verna Gateman slammed her apartment door, grabbed hold of the police whistle hanging from her neck and tried to blow into it while laughing at the same time.

CHAPTER IV

Sam Gateman had a regular morning ritual that consisted of stopping at Morris Cline's tailor shop before going to the district station house. Each morning, Morris Cline would press Sam Gateman's uniform for his morning inspection. Of course, Morris never charged his friend for pressing the uniform. It wasn't unusual for the little shops on an officer's beat to do little favors for him. And naturally, Sam Gateman didn't want to hurt anyone's feelings, so, he never turned down any kind of favor that was offered to him.

The little bell on the tailor shop door sounded it's alarm as Sam Gateman pushed the door open

"Good morning, Sam," greeted his friend as he pressed a pair of pants on his steam machine.

"Morning, Morris," Sam answered grumpily, "I've a favor to ask of you."

"Sure Sam. What is it?" asked the tailor.

Sam handed his friend the pair of police pants that his wife had sewed for him. Morris looked at the pants and started laughing. "You could never be a tailor, Sam," he said. "A cop you could be, but a tailor...never."

"Verna did that, Morris. Not me," Sam quickly informed his friend. "Can you sew them the proper way for me?" he asked.

"Sure, sure. I'll have them fixed for you in a jiffy. Sit down and relax. And while you're at it, take off your uniform. I'll press it for you. You've got a few wrinkles showing. How much time have you got before roll call?"

"Fifteen minutes, Morris," Sam answered as he removed his clothing.

"I'll have everything pressed in five minutes," boasted Morris.

Sam handed his jacket and pants to his friend. He the sat down in a semi-covered wooden cubical. He wore only his shirt, tie and police hat. Picking up the newspaper, Sam began to read to kill time.

"Let me have your gun belt and holster, Sam. I've a new cream polish that will make the leather shine like it was brand new."

Sam handed his utility belt to his friend, leaving his gun in the holster. "Be careful of the gun, Morris," he said. Morris laid the belt and holster down on the counter and brought out the new leather polish.

The bell on the shop's door signaled an entry into the tailor shop. Two young men, in their early twenties, entered the shop. Both were shabbily dressed: dirty jeans, ripped tee-shirts and uncombed straight black long hair. They quickly surveyed the surroundings in the shop. Sam Gateman paid them no attention. He continued to read the newspaper.

"Can I help you?" Morris asked as he continued rubbing the polish onto the utility belt.

"You sure can, pops!" said one of the young men, walking towards the shop owner. The young man quickly lifted his tee-shirt and removed a 45-automatic from his waist band. The other young man produced a revolver from his rear pocket and walked over to Sam Gateman.

"Come on out of that wooden cage cop and keep both of those hands of yours on that newspaper," ordered the young man.

"Now wait a minute," Sam protested, but his request was cut short.

"I said to come out of there!" the young man angrily ordered again. This time he pulled back the hammer on his revolver as he spoke.

"OK! OK! Just take it easy with that gun kid," Sam pleaded. He quickly followed the young man's instructions.

"What do you want with us?" asked Morris, still nervously polishing the gun belt.

"We want your money, pops," spoke the youth with the automatic," and don't touch that gun belt again."

Morris quickly backed away from the counter, raising his hands into the air.

"That's better," said the young man, picking up the gun belt. "*Now get that money,*" he shouted angrily.

Morris reached under the counter and brought up a battered cigar box. Opening it, he took out fifty dollars in old bills - - ones - - five's - - tens. He handed the money towards the young man.

"*Is that all the bread you got man?*" shouted the youth.

"That's all I have," replied Morris, shaking with fear. "I took all of the other money to the bank yesterday."

The young man grabbed the money and shoved it into his front pants pocket. He turned towards Sam Gateman. "All right cop," he snickered, "take off all of your clothes, except for your shorts and drop them on the floor in front of you."

Sam did as he was told, fighting desperately to keep his mouth shut. Both of the young men laughed when they saw Sam, wearing only his underwear, his hands raised in the air.

"Now stand back to back," ordered one of the youths. He found a piece of heavy cord in back of the tailor shop and tightly bound Morris and Sam together. When the young man was satisfied that the men couldn't untie themselves, he made Sam and Morris climb up on the counter and sit there.

"Let's have a little fun, Bernie," the youth remarked to his partner.

"OK," agreed the second youth, "go ahead and have your fun."

The youth picked up the telephone. "*What's the phone number of your station house?*" he shouted at Sam.

"Eight...nine...six...four...one...eight...eight," Sam replied, knowing what the youth was going to do.

"Get an empty garment bag and stuff his uniform into it, Bernie," said the youth with the automatic. He dialed the series of numbers Sam had given him and waited. "This is gonna be a blast, Bernie!" He laughed and jumped up and down on the floor.

"Forty-Third Precinct," said the voice on the other end of the telephone line.

"Hello," began the youth, "this is a concerned citizen calling. I just walked past Morris Cline's Tailor shop and there were two strange looking men sitting on top of the store counter. You had better send a squad car and sergeant over there right away to investigate."

Before the officer at the other end of the telephone line could say another word, the young man hung up the telephone. The other youth picked up the cloth garment bag containing Sam's uniform and they both ran out the front door, laughing hysterically as they ran.

Sam Gateman shook his head in total disgust. He knew he would be the total laughing stock of the entire district, once the word got around as to what had happened to him.

Verna Gateman vacuumed her living room rug. The shrill ring of the telephone startled her.

"*Sam*," she exclaimed, surprised to hear her husband's voice. "How come you're calling me so early in the day? You want me to bring you a change of clothes? Why?" she asked.

Sam began explaining his problem to his wife. Verna felt her stomach flip upside down as her husband revealed the entire embarrassing story. She could feel her blood pressure slowly rising.

Suddenly she remembered what her best friend had told her. She took hold of the whistle that was hanging from her neck, took a deep breath and blew as hard as she could into the mouthpiece of the whistle - - *Tweeeeeeeeeeeeeeeeeeeeeeet!*"

Sam Gateman dropped the telephone and placed his hands over his ears, trying desperately to stop the loud shrilling screech that echoed through his brain.

CHAPTER V

Verna finished washing the last of the dinner dishes. The rest of the family were relaxing in the living room. Sam Gateman was reading his newspaper, Sherry was reading a book and Dexter, well, he watched the evening news on the television set.

Sam set down his newspaper. "Kids," he began, speaking quietly, "we've got to do something about your mother and that damn whistle. All week long she's been driving me crazy with that thing. Every time I turn around, she's blowing into it."

"I know what you mean, dad," interrupted Sherry. "When ma wants me, she doesn't call for me any more. She blows three times on that darn whistle. Dad, why don't you hide it from her?"

"That wouldn't do any good, Sherry. Your mother would just go out and buy herself another whistle. Besides, she even wears that damn thing to bed with her. It's always around her neck."

"Hey, pop," interrupted Dexter, "why don't you get ma one of those high pitched dog whistles? Then no one would hear it."

"Your humor just isn't that funny right now ,Dexter," said Sam.

"Aw, why don't you two just leave ma alone," replied Dexter. "She'll be her old self in just a couple of days. This new game of hers will soon wear itself out."

"A lot you know mister big shot, "said Sam Gateman. "This is the first night this week that you've been home before 4 a.m. You haven't been around long enough to hear your mother and that damn whistle."

"Dad," whispered Sherry, "what's wrong with ma?" she asked.

"I believe your mother is going through a change of life cycle," answered Sam. "We've got to help her in every way that we can. Sherry, I think that if you brought some of your male friends home for dinner, that would probably help a lot. At least it would ease your mother's mind to know that you're going out with boys."

"OK dad, if that's what you want, I'll have a couple of my friends drop by for dinner a couple of nights."

Dexter picked up his cup of coffee and took a sip. Three loud shrieks suddenly came from the kitchen. Startled, Dexter dropped the cup of coffee into his lap. "What in the hell was that?" he asked.

Sherry stood up. "Don't be alarmed, Dexter," she said, "that call was for me. Ma wants me to help her wipe the dishes."

The sink was stacked with freshly washed dishes, pots and eating utensils. Verna Gateman was scouring a pot in the sink when Sherry entered the kitchen.

"You called, ma?" she asked.

"The dishes are ready for you to dry," said her mother.

"Ma, please don't blow that whistle when you want me," Sherry pleaded. "Just call out my name and I'll gladly come to see what you want."

"Hush," said Verna. "Don't argue with your mama. I've got a problem and Sarah Betz has helped me to solve it. I've got to blow this whistle. It's a great comfort for me."

"Not for when you're calling someone, ma," Sherry protested.

"I said hush girl! Now listen to your mama and wipe the dishes," ordered Verna.

Sherry tied a clean apron around her waist, picked up a pot and began wiping it with a dry dish towel. "Ma," she said softly while wiping a dish, "can I bring a friend home for dinner next week?" she asked.

"You can bring home who ever you want dear. Just let me know when, so I can make enough dinner for everyone and let me know what your girlfriends like to eat."

"It's not a girlfriend, ma," said Sherry, laughing, "it's a boy."

"*A boyfriend!*" shouted Verna, smiling from ear to ear. "When did you meet him? What does he do for a living? Who are his parents? Is he interested in marriage? You must be real sure of the man you are going to marry."

"Ma," Sherry interrupted her mother, "don't jump to conclusions. He's only a friend. I'm not in love with him."

"You never know, Sherry dear. You never know what can happen," said Verna, smiling. She began humming her favorite folk tune as she finished scrubbing the rest of the dirty pots. The well oiled wheels inside of Verna's brain began to revolve slowly. She was formulating a plan for capturing the right man for her daughter.

CHAPTER VI

As soon as the hands on the clock reached 6:00 a.m., the clock radio switched on. Verna quickly turned the radio off. She had already been up for an hour preparing breakfast for the rest of the family. The previous nights good news of Sherry's new male friend had excited Verna to the point of not being able to sleep.

The sound of clinking milk bottles came from the outer hallway. That must be Mr. Kenawski, the milkman, thought Verna. I've got to tell him the good news.

Edward Kenawski, a middle-aged man of fifty years, medium built, dark hair, a good personality, pleasant disposition, a little shy and on the nervous side, had heard from the neighbors about Verna Gatemans new gimmick with the whistle. He tried to deliver the milk as quietly as possible, trying to avoid a meeting or conversation with Verna Gateman.

Verna opened her front door just in time to see Mr. Kenawski delivering the milk at Sarah Betz's apartment door. Verna took a deep breath, put the whistle into her mouth and blew - - *TWEEEEEEEEEEEEEEEET*! The high shrieking sound bounced off of every wall in the long hallway.

Eggs, bottles of milk, butter and cottage cheese flew through the air, the containers cracking open when they hit the walls, ceiling and floor. Edward Kenawski felt as though he were ready to collapse from shock after hearing the piercing sound of the police whistle

"*Good morning, Mr. Kenawski,* "Verna shouted happily. "I've got some good news that I want to share with you this fine and lovely morning."

The milkman turned and looked up at Verna. "Please Mrs. Gateman," he pleaded, "don't ever do that again." He continued picking up the undamaged merchandise of his trade.

"My daughter has a boyfriend, Mr. Kenawski," Verna shouted again. "She's bringing him home for dinner one night next week. I think we'll be having a wedding soon."

"That's nice, Mrs. Gateman," answered Ed Kenawski disgustedly as he picked up the unbroken eggs off of the hallway floor.

Sarah Betz opened her apartment door, curious to see what the commotion was all about. She screamed when she saw the mess in the hallway in front of her apartment door. The milkman dropped all of his eggs again.

"*Sarah!*" shouted Verna, "I want you should come to my apartment later. I have some good news you should know. And, give Mr. Kenawski there a broom, mop and dust pan to clean up the mess that he made in the hallway. *Good-bye Mister Kenawski*," she shouted, then went into her apartment.

"Good-bye, Mrs. Gateman," sighed the milkman.

CHAPTER VII

Verna looked up at the clock hanging on the living room wall - - 6:15 a.m. She put the whistle in her mouth and began blowing it as she walked by each bedroom door. "*Everybody should get up now!*" she shouted, "*it's 6:15.*"

Three bedroom doors flew open, the occupants disbelieving Verna's latest method of waking them up in the morning.

"Ma...please! You've got to stop this," pleaded Sherry. "The neighbors were just complaining about you blowing that whistle at night and now you're blowing that whistle so early in the morning."

The telephone rang. Sam Gateman picked up the receiver. "Yes, Mrs. Stover, I know," he said into the receiver. "I'll see that she doesn't do it again." He hung up the receiver. "*Well, it's started, Verna! It's started again!*" he shouted. "You're going to have all of the neighbors calling and complaining again." The telephone rang again.

"You answer it this time, Dexter," Sam told his son, "you're never at home. You don't have to face the neighbors." Dexter picked up the receiver, said a few words and put the receiver back down. The telephone rang again... and again...and again.

"All the neighbors are calling and complaining about that damn whistle, ma," said Dexter.

"So let them call and complain, "said Verna, unconcerningly, "it'll do them good to get up early in the morning and see what the rest of the world looks like in the sunshine." She went back to her kitchen to finish making breakfast for her family.

The telephone rang again.

"Someone at the other end of the line wants to talk with a *SHORTS* Gateman," said Dexter, laughing as he spoke to his father. "They must mean you, pop!"

"Shut your mouth smart ass and get dressed," said Sam, grabbing the phone out of his son's hand.

CHAPTER VIII

The front doorbell rang. The entire Gateman family, except Verna, had left the apartment. Verna opened the door while munching on a cream cheese bagel. Sarah Betz stood waiting in the hallway. This time she was dressed in street clothes.

"So what's the big secret, Verna?" she asked. Verna, chewing a mouth full of food, motioned for her friend to enter her apartment.

"Sit down, Sarah," Verna finally said, "I'll get us some coffee and bagels to munch on."

"Don't forget the cigarettes," Sarah interrupted, "I left mine back in my apartment."

Verna went into her kitchen, shortly returning with a serving tray displaying cups, bagels, coffee and cigarettes.

"Verna," her friend began, "I think you should get rid of that whistle. It's causing quite a few problems in the building. I've heard several of the neighbors complaining about you. I even heard one person mentioning about having their own lynching party. Maybe that whistle wasn't such a good idea after all."

"Nonsense," said Verna. She poured two cups of coffee and handed her friend a cup. She continued. "It was a wonderful idea that you had. This whistle has helped me out many, many times. Everyone has been paying a lot more attention to me. But," she hesitated, "never mind about the whistle. Listen, Sherry has a boyfriend and she's bringing him home for dinner next week to meet her family."

"*A boy friend!*" exclaimed Sarah, almost dropping her coffee cup, "that's wonderful news, Verna. It's just what you wished for Sherry."

"Yes, and I can see a marriage in the near future."

"How can you be sure, Verna?" asked her friend.

"I know Sarah, believe me, I know," said Verna, shaking her finger from side to side at her friend. "Believe me, I know," she repeated. "Now, I want you should help me to plan a nice dinner for my future son-in-law."

"What kind of foods does he enjoy eating?"

"I really don't know." Verna hesitated. "But, I'll make him a fine Jewish meal. How could he not help but like it?"

"Well," Sarah paused, "why don't you start out with Lox, a cream cheese spread and crackers. Then, as a salad, serve the two-tone Gefilte fish mold on fresh green lettuce leaves. Some of your fantastic sauerkraut soup would be delicious after the fish mold. If you want to get fancy, put some Luckshen (noodles) in the soup. Then, have some hot Challah bread and butter with the meal. Now don't forget to make your cheese and mushroom matzo kugel too!" Sarah took a sip of her coffee then continued. "For the main dish, you can serve fish or beef and kasha. Rice filled artichokes would make a very fine vegetable to serve with the main dish. And finally for dessert, I would prefer the prune upside down cake. I would skip coffee with the meal. As he is still a growing boy, I would serve him some honey and banana milk for the dinner beverage."

Verna wrote down all of her friend's suggestions. "That's why I asked you to come over, Sarah. You've helped me make up my mind on what to serve for this special occasion. But, I still have another serious problem."

"What is it?" asked her friend, offering a sympathetic shoulder for her friend to cry on.

"I've got to make sure that Sherry picks the right man for her to marry. If she makes her own choice, I'm afraid that love might blind her and she might make a big mistake. It's up to me to see that see makes the right choice!"

"Have you thought just how you're going to go about doing it?" asked Sarah.

"Yes," said Verna, becoming very serious. "I've thought about that problem all last night. This is what I've decided to do. I'm going to use a grading system. I will give the boy points for each different stage of my test that he passes."

"Points?" said Sarah, puzzled. "How are you going to give him points?"

"Simple. I'll grade his actions on a scale of from one to ten. The system will work on every boy until I can find the right one for her. I'll grade them on their appearance, their choice of clothing, the greeting that they give to me when we first meet, the amount and kind of foods they choose and their families social status. The boy that scores the highest amount of points will be Sherry's husband and my new son-in-law!"

That's a very good idea, now that you've explained it to me, Verna. See, the whistle has made you think for yourself," said Sarah. She looked at her wrist watch. "*Oh*," she exclaimed, "it's ten after eleven already. I've got to hurry or I'll be late for my noon class."

"What class?" asked Verna, surprised by her friend's last statement. "What are you studying now?"

"I've signed up for a special handwriting course. Verna, you'd be surprised at what you could learn about a person's character just by studying that person's handwriting."

Sarah Betz stood up, put the pack of cigarettes into her pocket, bid her friend farewell and left the apartment.

CHAPTER IX

The alarm bell in the college corridor gave the signal for the students to change classrooms. Sherry Gateman walked into her English classroom.

Mark Fields was seated at the far corner of the room.

"Hi, Mark," she cheerfully greeted him as she approached.

"Morning, Sherry," he replied.

"Mark," she continued," would you please do me a great big favor if I asked you?"

"Sure," he replied without hesitation, "what is it?"

"It's my mother, Mark. She's all upset that I haven't brought any male friends home for dinner. She's all hopped up about me getting a boyfriend and then settle down to a nice quiet life. I'm not ready for that sort of stuff yet. I want to get my degree and then do some serious traveling. Maybe see what the rest of the world is like. I want to meet different people and see different things. Would you please come to dinner at my house next Tuesday night? You'd be doing me a big favor and making my mother happy. At least if she thinks I'm going with someone, she'll get off of my back."

"Hey...I'd love to come to dinner, Sherry," he replied enthusiastically. "What should I wear and what time do you want me at your house?" he asked.

"Just dress casually. Nothing fancy, but please be there at exactly 7:30 p.m.."

"Right! I'll be there with bells on my toes," he laughed.

"You're a life saver, Mark. Thanks a lot," she replied, throwing him a kiss with her hand.

CHAPTER X

Tuesday morning didn't come fast enough for Verna Gateman. When she reached the supermarket, it had only been opened an hour and already it was crowded with customers.

Grabbing an empty metal shopping cart, she took out her grocery list and quickly began her journey down the long aisles of endless cans, boxes and bags of various foods.

Within a half hour, her grocery cart was filled with the articles that she needed for her special dinner. She was still undecided as to what the main course would be - - fresh fish or meat?

Unhappy with the selection of meat that she saw on display, she decided that if she was going to get meat, the butcher would have to cut the meat special for her. She hesitated when she saw the fresh fish counter not far away from the meat display. She decided to examine the fish first before she bothered the butcher. She walked over to the fish counter.

How sad they all look, she thought to herself. Just laying on all that cold ice. She examined several pieces of fish and finally settled on twelve pieces of fish filets. The clerk weighed the fish for her, then wrapped them in freezer wrap paper. Verna placed the package in her cart and was ready to check out at the register when she saw a seven pound mackerel that caught her eye.

This fish would make a good meal Friday night, she thought. She picked up the fish to examine it more closely. The fish felt cold and slippery as she maneuvered it in her hands.

Two young children played tag, running up and down the long aisles, chasing each other. One of the children ran smack-dab into Verna Gateman, hitting her in the buttocks. Startled by the sudden impact, she screamed, sending the seven pound mackerel flying through the air.

The fish landed on a young women's neck. As the cold fish wrapped itself around the women's neck, she screamed and pushed her grocery cart forward. The cart bumped into a man who was bending over to get a can from the bottom shelves of the display. The man stumbled forward, falling into a group of cans stacked four feet high. Cans flew in every direction, making a large array of different noises.

An elderly woman carrying a small watermelon was hit in the hand by one of the flying cans. The melon fell from her hands, smashing into several pieces when it hit the floor. A young man running for the front door slipped on the watermelon juice and fell backwards into the cold storage case displaying hundreds of eggs in their cartons.

Other people shopping in the store became confused and started screaming, believing that something drastic had happened inside of the store. Most of the shoppers made a mad-dash for the exit doors.

Verna Gateman watched the mass confusion developing right before her very eyes. She felt that at any moment now she was going to scream out loudly. Her entire body became tense. She grabbed hold of the police whistle hanging from her neck, puckered her lips and blew into the whistle as hard as she could. More people screamed when they heard the loud shrill wail of the police whistle

The police arrived five minutes later. Verna Gateman was arrested for disorderly conduct and causing a riot. She was still protesting and blowing her whistle when the police escorted her out of the supermarket and put her into the back of a squadrol transport.

CHAPTER XI

"Verna, I don't know what in the hell I'm going to do with you?" shouted Sam Gateman as he and his wife entered the vestibule of their building. "It's a good thing the manager of the supermarket dropped the charges against you after I had a talk with him. You do realize that from now on, you are banded from ever going into that store again!"

"Don't worry your head Sam," she replied unconcerningly. "There are lots of other stores to shop in. Did you get all of the groceries that I had in my cart?' she asked.

"Yes, Verna," answered her husband, "I paid for everything that was in the grocery cart and the damages that you caused. I'll unload the car just as soon as I finish going to the bathroom."

The small clock on the top of the television set chimed 6:00 p.m. Verna rushed out of the kitchen and walked over to her divan. She searched frantically through several drawers. Upon locating what she wanted, she walked over to the couch, sat down and laid out several items on top of the cocktail table. She slipped several pieces of clean paper onto a clipboard, then picked up a ruler and pen and began drawing lines on the paper.

Sam Gateman, resting comfortably in his overstuffed chair, set down his newspaper. "When are we going to eat, Verna?" he asked. "I'm starved."

"We eat at 7:30," she answered, continuing to draw more lines on the paper.

"What in the hell are you doing now, Verna?" he asked annoyingly. Verna explained her point system for getting their daughter the perfect husband.

"*Oh, for Christ sake, Verna,*" Sam shouted. "Haven't you caused enough trouble for one day?" he asked. "Don't make any trouble for our daughter."

Verna set down the pen and ruler, tightly grabbed hold of her whistle and blew - - *Tweeeeeeeeeeeeeeeeeeeet!*

"OK...Verna...OK!" Sam shouted, throwing both his hands up in the air in submission and disgust. "Do what you want. Go ahead and make a fool of yourself. I wash my hands of this whole mess you're going to cause for our daughter." Sam picked up his newspaper and buried his face behind it. Verna smiled, remaining silent and went back to drawing more lines.

"Will Dexter be home for dinner tonight?" asked Sam, not bringing his face out from behind his newspaper.

"Dexter called earlier in the day He won't be home for dinner. He has a very important appointment at 7:30 tonight."

"I'll bet," Sam interrupted his wife, "that appointment is probably with a five foot seven inch blond who's built like the Golden Gate Bridge. And, I'll wager ten dollars that she has a jealous husband too!"

Verna grabbed her whistle and blew - - *Tweeeeeeeeeeeeeeeet!*

Sherry walked into the apartment just as her mother finished blowing her whistle.

"Thanks for the introduction, ma, "she remarked, "but next time, all you have to do is say that I'm home!"

CHAPTER XII

Verna walked nervously, pacing back and forth in the living room. She looked at the wall clock. 7:15 p.m. Sherry relaxed on the couch skimming through the pages of a magazine.

"Where is this boyfriend of yours, Sherry?" she asked.

"I told him to be here at exactly 7:30, ma. Take it easy. We still have fifteen minutes to go."

"Verna," Sam shouted from the back bedroom, "when in the hell are we going to eat? I'm starving."

"Soon...Sam...Soon," Verna answered. She went into the kitchen to check on her dinner.

Mark Fields idea of dressing casually was a sweat shirt with no holes in it, a clean pair of jeans, a new clean head band to hold back his long hair and a coat of clean polish on his toe nails that were showing through his open toed sandals.

He stopped at the Gateman's front door and pressed the doorbell button. Sherry jumped up, dropped her magazine on the couch, ran to the door and opened it.

"Hi, Sherry," he greeted her, smiling. "It's 7:30 on the dot and here I am!" He lifted his right foot and shook it. Ring-a-ting-a-ling rang the little bells attached to the front strap on his open toed sandals. "I told you I'd be here with bells on my toes," he said, jokingly.

Sherry didn't utter a single word. She didn't really appreciate Mark's bit of humor. She stood there, lymph and speechless. She stared wide eyed at Mark's sweat shirt. On the front of it, printed in big, black, bold letters was the slogan - - *MADE IN BED!*

"For Christ sake, Mark," said Sherry, almost at the point of hysteria, "I didn't mean for you to dress like this! Ma will freak out when she sees you dressed like that. You'd better leave before she comes in here and sees you."

Verna entered the living room just as her daughter finished speaking. She was ready to greet her perspective new son-in-law. Verna froze in her tracks when she saw Mark Fields standing in the doorway. Remaining silent, she slowly reached for her whistle.

"Ma, don't," Sherry pleaded. "Don't do it...not now... please!"

Verna released her grip on the whistle, waited a moment, then shouted as loud as she could, "*Sam*!"

CHAPTER XIII

Sam Gateman, Sherry and Mark Fields were seated at the dining room table. The setting of the table was picturesque perfect. It could have been a display in a home decorating magazine.

A white laced tablecloth covered the entire table. In the table's center was a crystal vase containing an array of freshly cut flowers. On each side of the vase was a silver candlestick holder, each holding a pure white candle. The dinner plates were made of the finest China porcelain and the eating utensils were made from the purest silver and gold.

Verna entered the dining room carrying a large silver tray. On it were the lox, cream cheese spread and crackers.

"We'll have an appetizer first," insisted Verna.

"For God's sake, Verna, you serve that while we're sitting on the couch, before dinner, not when we're seated at the dining table," said Sam.

"I know when we're suppose to eat these, "said Verna angrily, "as long as I went through the trouble to make these, we'll have them now." She walked over to Mark, held out the tray in front of him and waited for him to take a few crackers with her spread

"No thanks," declined Mark, "can't eat any of that stuff. I'm allergic to cream cheese."

Verna didn't say a word. She turned and went back into her kitchen without offering her husband and daughter any of the cream cheese spread. She set the tray down on the counter, picked up a pencil and clipboard and put a zero in the column labeled - - *Appetizers*.

She returned to the dining room carrying the two-tone Gefilte fish mold and set the dish on the dining room table.

"Have some Mr. Fields," she offered, "it's really very good for you."

"No thanks Mrs. Gateman," Mark declined again, "I break out in hives from eating Gefilte fish."

Verna made a quick retreat and went back into the kitchen, slowly developing an emotion of deep anger. She picked up the pencil and placed a heavy, black zero in the column labeled - - *Salad*.

He can't refuse my special soup, she thought as she carried the hot container of sauerkraut soup into the dining room. She placed the container on the table and filled Mark Fields soup bowl to the top before he could refuse her again. Mark picked up his soup spoon and tasted the hot soup.

"Best soup you've ever tasted, Mr. Fields?" she asked.

Mark Fields set his spoon down on the table and pushed the soup bowl to the side.

"The soup is to salty for me," he remarked, showing discontent at the taste of the soup.

Verna stormed into the kitchen, picked up the pencil and put two small, heavy black zeros in the column labeled - - *Soup*.

Sam Gateman and his daughter remained silent, just waiting for the volcano to explode.

Verna brought out the hot challah bread and noodles for the soup. She placed them on the table and went back into the kitchen without uttering a word to anyone. The next course of the meal to come out was the cheese and mushroom matzo kugel.

"How about some...," Verna stopped a moment, then began to speak again, "forgive me, I forgot! You don't like cheese!"

Mark Fields displayed a phony smile. He hadn't touched the noodles or the bread. Verna turned and went back into her kitchen. She picked up her pencil and put zeros in the columns marked - - *Noodles, Bread* and *Kugel*. She then drew a large *X* across the entire paper

"Mister Fields," she mumbled aloud, "it looks like you're a loser." She carried out the rice filled artichokes and placed them on the table.

"Now that really looks good, "said Mark. He placed three of the artichokes on his plate. Verna rushed back into the kitchen and placed a number 10 in the column labeled - - *Artichokes*.

Can't let him have a perfect zero, she thought to herself. She picked up the platter of halibut filets, stuck the pencil in her hair, tucked the clipboard under her arm and returned to the dining room.

"Some halibut, Mister Fields?" she asked, sitting down in her chair.

"No thanks, Mrs. Gateman." Mark declined her offer again. "I'll just stick with these artichokes. I'm a vegetarian ."

"A what?" asked a surprised Verna.

"A vegetarian," Mark repeated.

"Sam, come with me into the kitchen," ordered Verna as she stood up. Her movements resembled that of a top sergeant speaking to his men. Sam obeyed his wife without saying a single word and followed her into the kitchen.

"Mark, "said Sherry, "why didn't you tell me that you were a vegetarian?"

"That's simple, you never asked me," he replied.

Verna paced back and forth across the kitchen floor. "Sam,"she stuttered as she spoke, "you must tell that boy to leave our house. I can't have him in our house another minute." Verna unconsciously reached for her whistle.

"Leave that damn whistle alone, Verna," protested Sam, taking hold of his wife's hand. "We really haven't given the boy a fair chance. What's the difference if he dresses a little odd? Or, if he doesn't eat meat or fish. He probably has other traits that make him likable. Let's just give the boy another chance. Come on back to the table and let us all eat an enjoyable and quiet meal. OK, Verna?" he asked.

Verna forced a small smile and followed her husband back to the dining room table. They sat at opposite ends of the table. Verna placed a small portion of all the food on her plate. She wasn't really very hungry at the moment.

Mark Fields placed two more artichokes on his plate and consumed them rapidly. No other conversation was held during the rest of the meal.

After the basic meal was finished, Verna brought out the prune upside-down cake that she had baked. She also brought out a large cold pitcher of honey and banana milk. She cut a large slice of the cake and handed it to Mark.

"No thanks, Mrs. Gateman," he replied, "I don't care for any cake, but I will have a glass of that milk from the pitcher."

Verna wasn't about to tell him what was mixed in with the milk. She'd let him find out for himself.

He'd probably refuse that too if he knew what was in there, she thought to herself. She filled a large glass with the white liquid and set it down in front of Mark. As he lifted the glass, it slipped out of his hand and spilled on the table. Verna jumped up, frantic with worry. She quickly wiped up the liquid before it stained her best lace tablecloth and table top.

CHAPTER XIV

After they calmed Verna down, Sherry and Mark sat on the couch. Sam relaxed in his favorite chair again and started to finish reading his newspaper. Verna sat in a winged back chair with her clipboard resting on her lap.

"What's the clipboard for?" asked Mark.

"It's for an experiment that I'm conducting, Mister Fields," Verna answered coyly. "Would you mind if I asked you a few personal questions about yourself?" she asked.

"Mother...please... not now!" Sherry pleaded.

"That's all right, Sherry," said Mark, "I'd be glad to help your mother out with her project. Go ahead, Mrs. Gateman, ask your questions."

"First, Mr. Fields," Verna began, "what do you plan on doing with your life?"

"I plan on being as free as a bird, Mrs. Gateman," he answered without any hesitation. "I'll have no one to tie me down. I want to roam the earth where ever I please, whenever I please."

Frowning, Verna wrote down his answer on her sheet of paper. "Mister Fields," she continued, "how do you feel about marriage in general?"

Mark readjusted his body on the couch before he answered this question. "Marriage is all right for the other guy. Myself, I prefer to live common law with a woman. I can go as I please and she can do the same, and yet, we can still have a good sexual relationship together."

Sam Gateman stuck his head out from behind his newspaper and looked at his wife without saying a single word. Angry with Mark's answers, Verna's hand shook as she scribbled down his replies. She continued with her questioning. "How do you feel about having lots of children?" she asked

"*Shit...children! Not me, Mrs. Gateman,*"he shouted without hesitation. "If my common law wife had any children, why, I'd put them up for adoption right away! As I said, I don't want any rug rats bogging me down. I want to be free as a bird."

Verna jumped up from her chair. The clipboard went flying across the room. She grabbed hold of her whistle and took a deep breath.

"*No, ma. Not that... please!*" Sherry pleaded loudly.

Tweeeeeeeeeeeeeeeeeeeeeeeeeeet! The loud annoying sound filled the room. Sam dropped his newspaper when he stood up and tried to run out of the living room. Mark Fields jumped up off of the couch, disbelieving the sight that was developing before his very eyes.

Verna Gateman blew into her whistle - - again - - and again - -and again. Each time that she blew the whistle, she moved a little closer towards Mark Fields. He turned and tried to run for the front door, but he tripped over Sherry's foot.

"*I'll make you be as free as a bird,*" Verna shouted loudly, swinging her arms wildly in the air. "*And, I'll give you your own personal bird call too!*"

Tweeeet...Tweeeet...Tweeeet! Verna blew into the whistle repeatedly as she charged towards Mark, like a general going into battle.

"*Verna, cut it out!*" Sam shouted, grabbing hold of his wife's arms. "*Let the boy be!*"

Mark lifted himself off of the floor, ran to the door and opened it. "*You're nuts!*" he screamed. "*Nuts!...This whole family is crazy!*" He slammed the door behind him as he ran out of the Gateman apartment.

"Now look at what you've done, ma,"cried Sherry. "I'll be the laughing stock of the whole school when this gets around." She ran to her bedroom, crying hysterically

"Well, if I should say so myself, you've done it again, Verna," said Sam as he sat down in his chair. He picked up his newspaper from the floor.

"You've done it again," he repeated, shaking his head in disbelief.

CHAPTER XV

The following months passed quickly. A few of the officers at the district station still teased Sam, calling him *SHORTS* Gateman. Verna used her whistle more than ever. Even Sarah Betz started complaining about the noise. Sherry Gateman brought several more boys home for dinner, but her mother's whistle and clipboard kept them from coming back to the house. Dexter was doing badly in college, but he was doing great with the ladies.

The clock on top of the television set chimed 8:00 p.m. Sam sat in his favorite chair, reading his newspaper, as usual. Sherry laid on the couch reading the latest romance magazine. Verna stood in front of the television set turning the selector knob around and around, unable to decide on what program she wanted to watch.

Dexter came out of his bedroom wearing a pair of dark blue pants and buttoned a white dress shirt as he walked towards his mother. Verna stopped turning the selector knob and looked at her son.

"Going out again tonight?" she asked coldly.

"You know how it is, ma," he replied jokingly. "When you've got good looks, a wonderful personality and a good disposition, I see no good reason why I should be cooped up at home. I want to get around. I want everyone to enjoy my presence."

"Yea," Sam interrupted his son, "especially the women you go out with!"

"Hush, Sam," said Verna. "Dexter," she paused, "I noticed that your marks are not so good in school."

"Are you peeking at my mail, ma?" he asked jokingly. "You know that's a federal offense."

"I peek at no one's mail," she snapped. "I saw the notice from the college on your dresser when I was cleaning your room. When are you going to stay home and study so that you can pass your courses?"

"Don't worry about my grades," he answered as he tied his neck tie. "Everything will be OK. You'll see."

"The day after tomorrow is Thanksgiving. Will you be home to help us eat the turkey?" she asked.

"I really don't know, ma. I've got something hot brewing in the pot."

"I hope that pot doesn't have a husband," said Sherry, laughing.

"All kidding aside, ma," Dexter continued, "I've got a surprise for you and dad."

"A surprise?" exclaimed Verna. "What kind of a surprise?" she asked.

"You'll see when it gets here. It should be here tomorrow or the day after. I don't want to tell you anything more because it will ruin the surprise."

Dexter went back to his bedroom. A few minutes later he finished dressing and left the apartment. Nothing more was said about the surprise.

CHAPTER XVI

Thanksgiving morning had arrived. Everyone was still asleep except for Verna. She was working in her kitchen stuffing a large turkey with her special seasoned dressing. She looked at the clock when she finished tying the turkey with string to keep the dressing inside - - 8:45 a.m.

It'll take about six hours for this turkey to cook, she thought. We should be able to eat around 4:00 p.m. Verna placed the turkey in the oven and turned the selector knob to 450 degrees. She began peeling the potatoes.

The building to the left of the Gateman building had an apartment for rent. The local newspaper had made an error and printed the Gateman building and apartment numbers as being the apartment for rent.

A young, pretty girl, about twenty-five years of age, entered the vestibule of the Gateman building. She studied the ad in the newspaper again. The ad stated that the apartment that was for rent was on the third floor. The girl searched for an elevator, but there wasn't any. She began her long journey up the three flights of stairs.

Verna finished peeling the potatoes. Again, she looked at the kitchen clock - - 9:35 a.m.

I'll let them all sleep just a little while longer, she thought to herself. She picked up a large turnip and began peeling the wax covering off of it.

The young girl reached the third floor landing. She was breathing irregularly from the long climb up the stairs. Suddenly, she began to get terrible stomach pains. She looked around for someone to help her, but no one was up so early in the morning. She stopped at the Gateman's apartment door and pressed the doorbell button in desperation. The sound of the doorbell startled Verna.

That must be the surprise that Dexter told us about the other night, she thought to herself. She set the turnip and knife down on the counter top, wiped her hands in a towel, then went to answer the doorbell's call.

Upon opening the door, Verna was speechless and stood motionless when she saw the young girl. The girl's stomach was so large that it seemed it would burst if you touched it.

"I've got a nice surprise that's coming real soon," said the girl, her face filled with pain.

Verna wanted to speak, but she couldn't. Breaking into a cold sweat, Verna felt as if she was going to panic and run.

That son of mine, she said to herself, he has his baby delivered here to me even before its' out of the package! Verna grabbed her whistle, took a deep breath and blew - - *Tweeeeeeeeet!* A loud terrifying scream filled the hallway. Stunned and startled by the sound of the whistle, the young girl fainted.

At 9:45 a.m., in front of the Gateman's apartment door, a twelve pound twenty -five inch baby boy was born.

CHAPTER XVII

Sam Gateman entered the vestibule of his building. Two men were carrying a couch down the stairway.

"Excuse me," said one of the men as they squeezed passed Sam.

"Who's moving?" asked Sam.

Neither man answered him. They loaded the couch onto the back of a large van, closed the door and drove away. Sam Gateman shrugged his shoulders and walked up to the third floor of his building.

"*Verna ...I'm home,*" he shouted as he walked into his apartment.

"I'll be right with you, Sam" she answered from the kitchen. "Sit on the couch and relax."

Shortly after, Verna came into the living room carrying a large tray. On the tray were crackers, cheese, chopped chicken livers and a large glass container filled with gin and dry vermouth.

"What's all this?" asked Sam, surprised at the new change in his wife. Verna sat down on the couch next to her husband. She filled a cocktail glass and handed it to her husband. "I thought we'd have a few cocktails before our dinner, Sam" she said.

Sam sipped his drink, then spoke, "I'm glad you're getting back to normal, Verna. A couple more weeks with that whistle and I would have had to go and see a head doctor. By the way, I ran into two men carrying a couch out the front door. Who's moving?"

Verna picked up her glass. "Sarah Betz is moving," she answered nonchalantly.

"*Sarah Betz!*" Sam exclaimed. "Now my day is really complete. What ever made her decide to move?"

"The landlord," said Verna.

"The landlord?" remarked Sam, puzzled by his wife's answer. "I thought the landlord's wife and Sarah Betz were on very friendly terms."

"They still are. But, it was her husband who threw Sarah out of her apartment. Do you remember a few months back when I told you that Sarah was taking a new handwriting course in junior college?"

"Yea, I remember," said Sam. "What about it?"

"Well, it seems that Sarah analyzed the landlord's wife's handwriting. Sarah told the woman that she was overly aggressive, nervous and overly sexed. Her diagnosis was that the landlord's wife sleep in a separate bed and not have anymore sexual relations with her husband. The landlady told her husband, and, he got madder than hell and threw Sarah Betz out of her apartment."

Sam almost choked when he tried to drink and laugh at the same time. They both finished two more martinis.

"Will Sherry be home for dinner tonight?" asked Sam.

"No, she has some extra work to finish at school."

Sam smiled contentedly. "See how everything turned out, Verna. You don't have to worry about Sherry. She wants a career first, then she'll have her family."

"Yes Sam, I realize that now." Verna took another sip of her drink.

"And how about our Dexter's surprise," Sam continued. "I never dreamed that he would re-enlist into the Army and make it his career. I'm proud of him for his decision. After he finishes his schooling with the Army, well, anything can happen after that."

"You're right Sam," said Verna. She took another sip of her drink. "Everything has turned out wonderful."

"Do you feel all right, Verna, now that Doctor Melton has given you the proper medication for your problems?"

"I feel wonderful, Sam. I feel as if I were a young girl of twenty-five again." She giggled as she spoke.

"Are you absolutely sure, Verna?" Sam asked again.

"*Yes... Sam...Yes!*" she answered happily.

"*Good!*" Sam shouted. He took the whistle from around his wife's neck, placed it on the floor and stomped on it with his foot - - over and over again. The plastic crunched under the weight of his foot.

Sam set his empty glass down on the cocktail table and gave his wife a very seductive wink.

"Oh, Sam!" she exclaimed, "*it's only six o'clock!*"

HANS

CHAPTER 1

A dark blue station wagon sped rapidly down the dirt road, occasionally swaying from side to side, trying to avoid the various sized pot holes in the road. A small cyclonic cloud, created by the car's wheels, followed closely behind the station wagon.

Bill Ross was entering his barn when a series of loud blasts from a car horn stopped him in his tracks. The station wagon came to a screeching stop next to him.

Hans, Bill Ross's 150 pound silver and gray colored German Shepherd, came running out of the barn to see who had trespassed onto his master's property.

"Heel...Hans...heel...," ordered Bill Ross. The large dog stopped instantly, sitting at an erect position next to his master's side. Hans breathing was rapid as he filled with excitement, waiting for the intruder to come out of his car.

"Mornin Bill," came the greeting from the man sitting inside of the station wagon, "and how are you today, Hans?" he asked.

Hans, recognizing the intruder as a friend, began wagging his long furry tail.

"We're both fine this morning," answered Bill Ross as he smiled and softly stroked the top of Hans head with his the palm of his hand. "What's so important to bring you out here so early in the morning? Especially in your excited condition."

"Bill," began the man, hesitating before he spoke again, "he hit my stock again last night. Not only did he get the best of my herd, but Watkins and the Jamison herds too."

"What can I do about that, John?"

"Listen Bill, that cougar has to be stopped. In the past he would kill just to satisfy his hunger and fill his belly. But now, that cat kills for his own pleasure. He uses death to amuse himself. Between our three herds we lost ten cows last night."

"As I said before John, what do you expect from me? You and the other ranchers tracked down that cat once before and what happened? You lost him! If six ranchers, along with their hunting dogs, can't track down one cougar, how in the world do you expect me to catch him? No John, count me out." Bill Ross turned and walked into the barn. Hans followed closely behind.

"Wait Bill... Please wait," the man shouted as he ran into the barn after Bill Ross. "At least hear me out. Listen to what I have to say. Just give me five minutes of your time."

Bill Ross began feeding his dogs, going from cage to cage. Two years previous, he had decided on giving up raising cattle and decided on just raising dogs. By converting the barn into a large dog kennel, he had developed a successful business by breeding various types of dogs.

"Look John," interrupted Bill Ross. He hesitated and stopped feeding his dogs. "If you want to speak to me, you'll have to do it while I keep feeding these animals." Bill Ross continued filling the food trays with the solid granular pellets of food.

"Bill, we can't track down that cougar by ourselves. Every time we go after him the dogs freeze up when they get him boxed into a corner. They back off and the cougar gets away. Only once did we get a chance to take a shot at him, and then we missed him. You worked with dogs while you were in the army and with the K-9 unit when you were on the police force. To be perfectly honest, you and Hans are our only hope of ever getting that cougar. You've trained Hans into an excellent hunting dog and it's a known fact that he wouldn't back away from that cougar. Bill, I've been authorized to make you an offer if you'll agree to go after that cougar. The ranchers have come up with a nice amount of money."

Bill Ross finished feeding his dogs, set down the large bag of dog food and called Hans back over to his side. Stroking Hans head slowly, he looked at his friend.

"John, you're right about one thing. Hans wouldn't back away from that cougar. He'd stay with the cougar until either he or the cougar were dead. You said the other ranchers wanted me to go after that cat for them. Why should I? Two years ago when I was raising cattle, those same ranchers forced me to sell my cattle at a low market price. I almost lost everything I had. But, I managed to make it through my crisis. Not one of those ranchers offered to help me out."

"I had nothing to do with that, Bill," interrupted John Tenner.

"I know you didn't, John. You were one of only a few people that tried to help me out of my dilemma. How much are they offering for me to catch the cougar?"

"Twenty-five hundred dollars," John Tenner replied instantly. Bill Ross continued stroking Hans head as he spoke.

"Tell you what, John. If you raise that offer to ten thousand dollars, you've got yourself a deal! That's the amount I lost on my cattle two years ago."

"I'll make up the difference myself, Bill," answered John Tenner. "It also means a lot to me if that cougar is killed."

"Suit yourself, John. We've got a deal." The two men shook hands. "But there's only one other condition to our deal."

"What's that?" asked John Tenner.

"I don't think it will take me more than two days to track that cougar down and kill it. I'll need someone to take care of my dogs while I'm gone."

"That's no problem," said John Tenner, smiling. "I'll have my son drive up to your place twice a day to feed and exercise your animals."

"Then it's settled, John. I'll get ready. It'll take me about an hour. I want to get started while that cougar's trail is still hot and his scent is strong."

The October air was crisp and cold. Large dark grayish-black clouds passing over the countryside gave notice that snow was coming soon. John Tenner got into his station wagon, wished Bill Ross good luck on his hunting venture, then drove away.

"Come along, Hans," said Bill Ross, "you've got a busy two days ahead of you. Let's go into the house and get packed so we can be on our way." Hans rapidly wagged his tail back and forth, barking excitedly as he followed his master into the small white house.

II

Bill Ross filled his canteen; half with water, the other half with his favorite aged brandy. The water would satisfy his thirst and the brandy would take the sting out of the cold night air. He packed enough rations in his knapsack to last him and Hans three days. Fresh ammunition was put into his cartridge belt. He checked his rifle over carefully making sure that is was in perfect working order. Hans rested on the living room floor, watching every move that his master made.

When Bill Ross removed his hunting boots from the front hall closet, Hans knew where they were going. He got up off of the floor and nervously pranced back and forth at the front door. Hans eagerness caught his master's attention. Bill Ross smiled, then spoke. "Don't worry Hans, we'll be on our way shortly. I've just a few more things to gather."

Fifteen minutes later they walked out the front door of the house. Hans jumped into the back seat of his master's car. Bill started the car, then drove down the dirt road, heading straight for John Tenner's ranch.

As Bill drove along, he thought, the best place to start tracking the cougar is where he killed his last victim. A quarter of an hour later they reached John Tenner's ranch. Three mutilated carcass still lay on the blood stained grass. Small animals had already started feeding off of the dead cattle. They scampered into the woods when they heard the sound of Bill Ross's car approaching them.

As soon as the car stopped, Hans jumped out of the open car window and began sniffing the ground excitedly. Within minutes, Hans picked up the cougar's scent and was anxious to go after the intruder.

"Good boy, Hans," said Bill, laughing as he spoke. "Make sure you've got the right scent. We don't want him getting to far of a head start on us."

Hans barked several times, then made a mad dash towards a large group of trees that were surrounded by heavy underbrush..

"Hold on Hans," Bill shouted, as he put his knapsack on his back. He clipped his canteen onto his belt, then picked up his rifle. "I'll be right there with you."

The German Shepherd and his master made their way through the thickly wooded area. Hans managed to stay fifteen feet in front of his master. The overhead clouds darkened with each minute that the clock ticked away the minutes. Bill looked at his wrist watch. Two p.m. They had only traveled four hours. Because of the thickness of the underbrush, it seemed as though they were traveling twice as long.

"Come here, Hans," beckoned Bill Ross, "it's break time. Let's take a few minutes to eat and rest. We've still a long way to go."

Although he was anxious to continue on, Hans obeyed his master's command, coming to rest at his master's feet. Unbeknown to Bill Ross, the cougar's scent was getting stronger to Hans. Whether it was carelessness or just his reassurance of knowing that no one was going to follow him made the cougar sloppy in his escape.

Bill chewed on a small piece of beef jerky. He shared his small ration supply with Hans. He also gave Hans a few dog biscuits as a special treat. The rifle was checked again making sure that it was still in good working order. The dampness and cold made the grease and lubricating oil on the weapons moving parts thicken, making most of the moveable parts work sluggishly. Bill maneuvered the slide bolt back and forth causing friction to warm the oil. There was no way on earth he wanted to come face to face with that cougar and not have his rifle working properly.

Finishing the last of the beef jerky, Bill washed it down with a drink from his canteen. His meals had to be minimal because a bloated feeling would slow him down.

"OK Hans," he began, petting his dog, "time we got started again. You take the lead. You're more anxious to meet up with him than I am."

Hans sniffed the leaf covered ground and located the cougar's scent immediately. The winds had picked up momentum, tearing the remaining leaves loose on the almost naked trees. From the direction they were headed, Bill deduced that the cougar was heading for Clausers Mountain.

Bill stopped walking. Not hearing his master's footsteps behind him, Hans stopped too. Bill checked his wrist watch. It was now 5:30 p.m.

"Well Hans, we've been traveling for seven and a half hours. We should be catching up with that cat soon."

Hans cheerfully barked in approval and ran off towards the underbrush approximately fifty yards to the left of his master. Hans suddenly stopped next to a large oak tree. He began to bark furiously. Bill couldn't imagine what Hans had discovered. He lowered his rifle and cautiously walked towards the oak tree.

On the ground before him laid the torn carcass's of a female deer and her young offspring.

"Easy Hans... Easy boy... Just take it easy and rest here awhile." Hans obeyed his master, laying down on top of the dead oak leaves scattered about the ground. Bill walked over to the dead deer, bent down, then touched the female deer's motionless body. Blood was still trickling out from the animal's wounds. It was still warm.

The blood hasn't had a chance to clot yet, thought Bill. She's only been dead a short while. That cougar can't be to far away.

A loud terrorizing cry of anger filled the emptiness of the forest that surrounded them. Hans quickly stood at attention. He remained perfectly still -- just listening. His ears stood straight as he stared in the direction of Clausers Mountain.

"That's not the wind, Hans. That's the cat that we're chasing. The cougar's caught our scent. That loud cry was just a warning to let us know that he's waiting for us. He's challenging us Hans. Let's not keep him waiting to long."

It began to snow. The tiny liquid crystals pinched Bill's face as the wind blew them wildly against it. As Bill and Hans trudged along, the cougar would occasionally scream out his warning of defiance and boldness.

The falling snow, covering the ground, resembled a large white blanket. Bill and Hans had traveled another ten minutes, when they spotted the cougar standing majestically on a rock ledge, some 200 feet above them. The cougar showed his white, sharply pointed teeth and shrieked loudly, hoping to scare the two intruders who had invaded his realm.

Hans anxiously waited for the moment when his master would give him the command to attack the cougar. He pranced nervously, back and forth in front of Bill, waiting for that special attack signal.

"Stand easy, Hans," whispered Bill. "We're getting close to his den. He doesn't want us to go any farther." Bill lifted the rifle butt to his right shoulder, took careful aim through his scope and squeezed the trigger slowly. The rifle bolted against his shoulder as the sound of a loud explosion echoed throughout the forest sanctuary.

The cougar shrieked and flew into the air, disappearing behind the rock ledge.

"*WE GOT HIM, HANS!*" Bill shouted excitedly. "Let's go up and pick up the carcass!"

Hans and his master started up the rocky terrain. A vision above them momentarily stopped them in their tracks. The wounded cougar reappeared on the rocky ledge. He was angrier and more defiant now then he had been before. Again Bill took aim with his rifle. Before he could get a chance to fire his weapon again, the animal disappeared from view.

"We only wounded him, Hans. We've got to kill him now for sure. He'll be more dangerous than before, now that he's wounded."

Bill and Hans finally reached the top of the rocky ledge. Hans sniffed the ground, quickly picking up the cougar's scent again. Bill located several drops of blood on the ground that showed the cougar's escape route.

"Stay here with me, Hans," Bill said sternly. "He's headed for his den. You'll get your turn at him soon enough. We'll follow the drops of blood. It shouldn't be long before we find his home."

Crimson circles on the white freshly fallen snow made a perfect trail for them to follow. On the side of the mountain, some 500 feet away from the rocky ledge where the cougar was wounded, grew a large cluster of heavy brush. The bloody trail lead straight into the middle of the twisted cluster of branches.

Cautiously, Bill and Hans approached the branches. No sounds or movement came from within. Bill pushed aside some of the wooden stems with the tip of his rifle. A hole, big enough for a man to walk through, appeared on the side of the mountain.

"Hans, we've got to be very careful from now on," whispered Bill, as they cautiously entered the entrance leading into the large rock formation. Bill's vision was limited to only the entrance to the cave. Darkness was dominant. He picked up a thick branch, pulled out a torn piece of shoe lace from his jacket pocket and tied some dried leaves and twigs to the wooden stem. Taking a match out of his front pants pocket, he lit it and ignited the leaves. It made a perfect torch.

Bill briefly surveyed the walls of the cave. Heavy timbers held the walls and ceiling of the cave in tact.

"Well, I'll be damned," Bill mumbled loudly, "it's an old mine. I didn't even know it existed."

Hans and his master walked approximately ten feet into the tunnel, then stopped. They had to make a quick decision. The tunnel's main entrance now divided into two other tunnels. Hans sniffed the ground in the tunnel on the left, then did the same thing to the tunnel on the right. The cougar's scent was in both of the tunnels. Hans was confused.

"Having a little trouble, Hans?" asked Bill. "That's O.K. You did a fine job tracking him this far. He's been in both of these tunnels at one time or another. We'll have to rely on my judgment from now on." Hans master let the knapsack drop off his back. "I'll leave this here for now. I don't want anything hampering us when we come face to face with that cougar." Hans barked in approval.

III

The tunnels reeked of mildew, rotting animal carcasses and animal wastes. Thick cobwebs connected the ceiling with the walls. Bill decided to check out the tunnel on the right first.

"Stay close to me ,Hans," he said as he started moving along slowly," no telling what we'll run into."

Bill held his crudely constructed torch out in front of him, just above his head. Hans walked slowly, just in front of his master, taking caution with each footstep he took.

They had walked a hundred yards into the tunnel, when the tunnel took a sharp turn to the right. The quick movement of a rat made Hans stop. The rat scurried into the new tunnel with Hans following closely behind. The dog's unexpected movement startled Bill Ross.

"*COME HERE, HANS!*" he shouted, running after his dog. Unaware of the large rock formation covering the center of the dirt floor, he tripped over it. The torch fell out of his hand. As his knees hit the ground, his finger squeezed the rifle's trigger. A loud explosion echoed throughout the tunnel as a small metal projectile bore its' way into the tunnel's ceiling. The loud vibrations immediately released tons of rock and dirt that covered the floor and blocked the tunnel. In a matter of seconds, Hans was trapped in the small tunnel...just him and the rat. There was no way out for him. The new tunnel only extended ten feet into the side of the mountain

Bill covered his head with his arms, trying to protect his head from the falling rocks and dirt. Rock after rock bounced off of his body. A few moments later, everything was quiet again. Bill coughed. The stirring dust seemed to leap into his lungs with each breath that he took. Total darkness surrounded him. Crawling on the floor, Bill felt his way around with the touch of his hands. He succeeded in locating his crudely made torch. His body, aching with pain, seemed to be all intact. Slowly he reached into his front pants pocket and removed a book of matches. He felt the attached contents between the two pieces of cardboard.

Only two matches left, he thought to himself, got to make sure I light the torch on my first try. His hands felt wet and sticky. His fingertips seemed to stick to the matchbook cover. Removing one match, he struck it on the base of the match cover. A flame appeared. He was blinded momentarily

Never would, he thought, the glow of a burning match look so good to me. He touched the lit match to the torch. It immediately caught fire. Holding the torch above his head he surveyed the area that he was trapped in. By some dumb luck, some of the old beams above his head held fast and prevented him from being buried alive. A huge mound of dirt and rocks sealed off the tunnel, behind and in front of him.

Surveying the small confining area, he located a convenient spot to place the torch. Jabbing the end of the torch into the ground, he placed rocks around the base of the stick. He kept stacking the rocks until he was sure that the torch wouldn't fall over.

Finally, he sat down and rested. He felt helpless and exhausted. Bill placed the back of his head against the damp tunnel wall. For the first time since the cave in, he thoroughly checked his arms and legs. His jacket and shirt were both blood soaked. Slowly removing the jacket, he tore open his shirt sleeve. A sharp piece of falling slate had cut through his jacket and shirt, placing a four inch gash in his forearm and wrist.

A throbbing sharp pain shot upwards from the calf of his left leg. Upon examining his leg, he saw a piece of timber sticking into the flesh. Slowly, but carefully, he removed the piece of wood, trying not to leave splinters inside of the wound. The piece of wood had just started to penetrate the leg muscle, but didn't go in deep enough to do any real damage. Sliding his pant leg up over the wound, he again examined it. Of what he could see by the torch light, dirt had already entered the wounds on his arm and leg. He removed his shirt and his tee-shirt. The tee-shirt was made of white cloth and would make a good wrapping bandage.

For the first time, he had felt the cold and dampness that dominated the inside of the tunnel. Bill quickly put on his shirt, giving his body a little protection from the cold. Removing the canteen off of his belt, he unscrewed the cap and poured some of the precious liquid into the wound on his leg. Tearing the tee-shirt into strips of cloth, he tightly tied a crude bandage over his leg wound.

The pain in his wrist and forearm ached more than his leg wound. He poured more of the precious liquid over his arm. At first it felt good, but when the water and alcohol mixture reached the inner part of the wound, it began to sting. Bill grit his teeth together as the burning sensation became more intense. At last the pain subsided. Bill examined his arm again. The wound was clean of dirt but it was still bleeding. Combining several strips of cloth from the tee-shirt, he made a compress and placed it over the wound, then tied the other strips of cloth tightly around his arm.

"That'll slow down the bleeding," he mumbled to himself. Again he surveyed his captive chamber. He estimated the area to be approximately ten feet wide, fifteen feet long and eight feet high.

A reasonably large enough area, he thought. Suddenly, one single word began running through his mind.

"*ESCAPE!*" he shouted loudly, "I've got to find a way out of here." His dog... Where was Hans... Was he O.K... Was he still alive?

"*HANS! HANS! ARE YOU O.K.?*" Bill shouted loudly. Remaining motionless, he had hoped to hear any kind of sound from his dog. He remained quiet and continued listening. No reply came from Hans

He's gone, Bill whispered, he's got to be buried under all of that dirt and rock. A strange feeling suddenly dominated him. Which way was his way out of this prison?

Bill began digging at one of the large mounds of dirt, hoping to find some kind of an opening, any kind of a clue for a way out. He found nothing! He slid over to the other mound of dirt that sealed him in the tunnel. He began to dig. Again, no opening or clue to a way out was found. Bill had lost all sense of direction. He had to make a quick decision. Which mound of dirt would be the best to start digging to find his way out?

The choice was made. Bill began to dig with his good arm. He resembled a dog trying to dig up an old bone. He removed rocks and scooped away hands full of dirt.

An hour had passed . Bill really wasn't making any progress. As he removed rocks and dirt, more dirt and rocks fell from the tunnel's ceiling, filling up the hole that he had just cleared out.

I've got to construct some kind of a support for the ceiling, he thought. I've got to dig a small tunnel that's big enough for me to crawl through. The mountain may come down on me, but it's a risk that I have to take.

Bill gathered what pieces of wood that he could find and stacked them neatly on a pile. Figuring that his confinement would be for quite some time, he searched his pockets to see what provisions he had and what items he could use as digging tools.

Everything that he owned was placed on the ground before him - - one candy bar, twelve live cartridges, the canteen with less than half of its' precious liquid, a handkerchief, one set of car keys, a match book with one match left, one pack of cigarettes containing three cigarettes, a wallet and sixty-five cents in United States coins.

Not much to work with, he thought. That candy bar and liquid have to last me until I can dig my way out of this place. The first thing I must do is keep a fire going for light and warmth.

His captive chamber began to fill with smoke from the torch. Only peculiar thing was that there wasn't much smoke from the torch. Bill struggled lifting himself off of the ground. He examined the solid rock walls. It wasn't long before he located a two inch crack in one of the rock walls. Picking up the torch, he placed it next to the crack. The flame from the torch leaped wildly into the crack.

"A draft," he shouted happily, "that's where the rest of the smoke is going. It's being sucked out of here! The crack is working like a giant vacuum cleaner. It must go through, connecting itself with the other tunnel. At least I'll have fresh air."

Bill finished examining the rest of the rock walls. He deduced that it was impossible for him to cut through that solid rock. At the base of the large crack in the wall, he jammed the end of the torch into the dirt floor. Smoke from the torch slowly drifted upwards until it reached the middle of the crack, then disappeared as it leaped into it.

One more problem solved, thought Bill. His head began to ache. Rubbing his fingers gently over his forehead, he located a large bump on the right side. Must have happened when those rocks were falling, he mumbled.

Looking at his wrist watch, he saw that the glass crystal was broken. The little metal hands were also bent out of shape. Shaking the watch for a moment, he held it up to his ear and listened. There was no sound... No ticking. Angrily, he squeezed the watch in his hand and threw it against the rock wall, smashing it into several pieces of worthless material.

"Better start digging again if I'm ever gonna get out of here," he said aloud. Bill selected a pointed piece of broken timber with his injured hand and immediately dropped it. His arm ached with pain. All the digging would have to be done with his good arm. This didn't help his situation, especially since he was right handed.

Dropping to his knees, he picked up the piece of wood and started stabbing at the large mound of dirt again.

IV

The amount of blood that he had lost had weakened him without him even realizing it. After digging for two hours and successfully tunneling twelve inches into the mound of dirt, he fainted and rolled down onto the dirt floor. At first when he awoke, Bill couldn't remember where he was. Then the realization that he was trapped in a tunnel brought him back to reality. He slowly lifted his head off of the ground. Total darkness dominated the small chamber.

"*THE TORCH!*" he shouted, "*WHERE IN THE HELL'S THE TORCH!*" Panic stricken, he forced himself up off of the dirt floor and felt his way in total darkness until he found the crack in the wall. Looking into the crack, he strained his eyes until he saw a faint ray of sunlight.

I must have slept all night, he thought. I wish I knew what time of day it was. Knowing that he only had one match left, he decided on sitting in total darkness and resting, maybe catch a little more sleep. The more sleep he got, the less he would be tempted to finish his one candy bar and the rest of his precious fluid in the canteen. Bill decided that when he couldn't see daylight at the other end of the crack, he would then make another fire. He had to get in all of his sack time now. He couldn't afford to fall asleep and let the fire go out again.

Sitting back down on the ground, he rested his head against the rock wall, closed his eyes and fell fast asleep again.

V

Sharp hurting pains in his stomach woke him up. Hunger pains, he deduced to himself. Taking the candy bar out of his coat pocket, he ripped away some of the paper wrapper and took a few small bites. Unscrewing the cap off of his canteen, he placed the opening of the metal container to his lips. Taking two long swallows he said, "God that's good." When he was finished he rescrewed the cap onto the neck of the canteen and placed it back on the ground. He felt weak - - cold - - and hungry. Forcing himself up again, he felt his way along the rock wall until he located the large crack again. Bill strained his eyes trying to see any rays of sunlight. They weren't there. Nothing was there.... Nothing but total darkness.

Must be night time again, he mumbled. Mind as well get that fire started. Feeling his way in the dark, Bill managed to gather some pieces of wood and piled them under the large crack in the wall. Taking his candy wrapper, he lit his last match and ignited the paper. Quickly and hopefully, he placed the burning paper under the small pile of wood.

"*COME ON YOU SON-OF-A-BITCH! CATCH ON FIRE!*" he shouted loudly, pounding his good fist on the cold, damp ground, "*DON'T FAIL ME NOW! BURN WOOD! BURN!*"

The small flickering flame leaped upward into the center of the small wood pile. Shortly, the captive chamber was aglow with flickering light from the burning embers.

"*YAHOO!*" Bill Ross shouted happily. He fell to the ground again. He felt weak. More rest was needed. He could feel the pulse beat of his heart throbbing in his arm and leg wounds. The pain had again become unbearable. He had no choice but to suffer with it. The bandages had turned to a solid crimson red color. The bleeding had seemed to stop.

Mind as well continue my digging on the escape route that I started, he thought. His heart felt as though it would leap out of his body when he looked at the small tunnel that he had started digging. At sometime during his sleeping period, his makeshift tunnel had collapsed. He felt lost. Trapped. The feeling of panic wanted to overtake control of his mind.

"*CALM YOURSELF, BILL!*" he screamed. "*CALM YOURSELF!*" Stabilizing his wits, he began to think clearly once again. Bill examined the tunnel's ceiling. Talking aloud seemed to calm him. "If I could start digging at the top of the dirt mound, it might be possible for me to construct some kind of support up there."

Picking up several pieces of wood, Bill started his digging venture again. For some unknown reason, the digging went easier this time. Rocks and pieces of timber held up his ceiling as he dug.

After digging for hours, Bill successfully constructed a two foot long tunnel. The digging had made his fingers raw. His body ached with pain from the awkward position that he had to be in to dig. It was time to stop the digging. He had to rest. Sliding down the dirt pile, he rested on the ground. The fire began to flicker. The brightness of the flames seemed to be getting dimmer. Bill threw a few more pieces of wood onto the burning embers. Within minutes the chamber was again aglow with a bright, warm light. The hunger pains came again. He must eat to keep up his strength.

The last piece of his candy bar tasted good. He took a drink from his canteen. Holding the canteen in his hand, Bill stared blankly at the rock wall.

How long have I been trapped in here? He thought to himself. One day... Two days? How long was I unconscious? He tried to force the thoughts from his mind. He again began to feel helpless and depressed. He had to go back to his digging.

Four more hours had passed. He suddenly heard a strange sound. He stopped digging and listened. It sounded like the cry of a small baby. Was it Hans? He thought. Was he still alive? Was he digging in the wrong direction to gain his freedom? If he was... so what. As long as Hans was alive he would be good company for him.

Bill stabbed and jabbed at the dirt until he broke through to the other side of the dirt mound. With the grace of God, the rocks in the tunnel's ceiling had locked themselves together, keeping more rocks and dirt from falling. Bill stared into the pitch darkness of the other tunnel. He saw no sign of any movement.

"*HANS!*" he shouted excitedly, "*IS THAT YOU BOY? IS THAT YOU?*" Again he heard a soft whining cry. "*HANS, IS THAT YOU?*" he called once more. Total silence followed his second call.

It's got to be him, thought Bill. Then the thought occurred to him that his dog did not have anything to eat or drink for several days. He poured some of the liquid from his canteen into the palm of his hand, then placed his hand through the small opening

"Here Hans," he said, then whistled. "Here's some water for you boy," he said quietly. No friendly greeting came from the other part of the tunnel. Instead, an angry, confused, hungry and terrorizing growl came from the new part of the tunnel. It was a sound of fear.. .a sound of warning...a warning that an attack was going to happen at any second.

The scent of the water and blood mixture on Bill's palm drove the poor dog to the point of hysteria. The sounds Bill Ross now heard were the sounds of a wild, savage beast. The reality of what was about to happen finally struck Bill. Hans had reverted to his wild animal instincts for survival. Attack - - and - - Kill!

The large German Shepherd's jaws anchored themselves onto Bill's arm. The lack of food and water had dominated the dog's sense of reasoning. Repeatedly, the sharp pointed teeth plunged deeply into Bill's arm. What was happening seemed unreal. Bill couldn't believe that this was happening to him. Frantically, he tried to pull his arm out of the small opening, but the dog's strong hold onto his arm was just to much for him.

Hans savagely swung his head from side to side: growling, pulling and tugging, until a hunk of flesh and muscle ripped off of Bill's arm. Bill pulled his arm out of the small tunnel. He caressed it against his chest. He was in total pain. The precious red fluid that kept one's body alive was now flowing out of the wound, falling freely into the dirt floor.

Bill quickly tore a piece of cloth off of the bottom of his shirt and tied it tightly around the top of his arm. Picking up a piece of wood, he preceded to make a tourniquet. Hans had now tasted warm blood and eaten human flesh. To him, it was fresh food - - and he wanted more.

Hans charged up the dirt mound trying desperately to stick his head through the small opening. Savagely, he clawed at the small opening with both his paws, trying to make the opening larger

Bill knew that it was only a matter of hours before Hans would come rushing through the opening. He tried to push a small boulder up the mound of dirt, hoping to block the opening. The pain in his arm was too unbearable. Bill's energy finally was gone. He collapsed on the ground.

VI

Bill slowly opened his eyes. The light from the burning timber had diminished again. The angry sounds of desperation and hunger could be heard as Hans continued his digging.

His arm had stopped bleeding. Lifting himself off of the ground, he felt weaker. Stumbling from dizziness, Bill caught his balance and rested against the rock wall. He threw several more pieces of wood onto the fire. There wasn't much wood left. The hungry flames leaped at the new pieces of kindling. The tunnel filled with light again. For how long, Bill didn't know.

Hans nose could now be seen coming through the hole. He had to find some way to stop the dog. An idea came to him. Picking up six of his cartridges, Bill decided on using the powder inside of them. One by one, he placed the tip of each bullet into the small part of the crack in the wall and maneuvered the bullet back and forth. The tips were eventually loosened and he was able to remove all the powder from the metal casings. Dumping the cigarettes out of the cigarette pack, he placed all the powder into the empty pack. Twisting the top of the pack tightly, he placed the pack into the small tunnel's opening. Picking up a small piece of burning timber, Bill placed the burning wood next to the cigarette pack. He quickly slid down the dirt pile and hid in the furthest part of his prison chamber for protection.

Within minutes, the powder ignited. A large pop, followed by a bright flash and a large cloud of smoke filled the tunnel.

Hans backed away from the small opening, shrieking from both pain and surprise.

That should hold him for awhile, thought Bill. What do I do now? How do I get out of here before he gets to me? Questions? To many unanswerable questions clouded his mind.

Hans vision was quickly restored to him. The bright flash had only blinded him momentarily. He was determined now, more than ever, to get on the other side of the mound of dirt. It wasn't just hunger that drove him onward, there was now an enemy that he had to kill.

Hans charged the opening repeatedly. His paws moved faster and dug deeper than they had before. Anger and rage gave Hans additional strength to keep on going.

Bill sat on the ground feeling totally helpless. Hunger, cold, dampness, and fatigue were also his enemies now. Hans entire head could now be seen through the opening.

Bill Ross had indeed picked the wrong direction to gain his freedom. That wrong choice was going to bring him death from an animal whom he had loved and trusted. There was only one answer left. He had to start digging at the other side of the tunnel. His only salvation was to dig straight through the pile of dirt and stones without running into any obstacles.

The light in the tunnel was diminishing again. Bill lifted himself up and stumbled from dizziness again. He swayed from side to side, making his way towards the stack of burning timbers. He threw all, but one piece of the remaining pieces of wood onto the fire. His one board would be needed for digging. Saving the rest of the wood wouldn't do him any good once Hans broke through the opening.

Bill dropped to his knees and started stabbing the pointed piece of board into the dirt pile. Surprising enough, this mound of dirt seemed easier to dig through. The ceiling and walls of the new tunnel held fast. The rocks that had fallen from the ceiling had stacked themselves in a formation, one on top of the other, forming a small archway. All Bill had to do was scoop that dirt away and he would be home free. This time, just by sure luck, he had picked the right spot to do the digging.

VII

Working on the new tunnel for almost an hour, Bill succeeded in breaking through to the other side of the wall of dirt. A small ray of sunlight found its' way through the opening.

Daylight already, thought Bill. But what day was it? Confused, he shook his head from side to side, trying to clear his head. He had to get things organized in their proper perspective inside of his mind.

He jabbed his board into the pile of dirt again. A loud shrill scream filled the entire tunnel. What had he hit? He pulled the board back, touching the tip with his fingers. The tip was wet - - tacky - - red in color.

"Blood," said Bill, "it's got to be blood." The agonizing scream came again, followed by the sound of digging.

"*THE COUGAR!*" shouted Bill, "*I'VE STABBED THAT GOD DAMN COUGAR!*"

Within minutes, the head of the cougar could be seen coming through the new opening. Anger and rage shown clearly in the beast's eyes. Saliva dripped freely from the corners of his mouth as he tried furiously to force his shoulders through the small opening.

Bill sat on the ground. Panic began to overcome his wits. He wanted to stand up and just run! Where could he go? There wasn't even a rock large enough for him to hide behind. Both animals would eventually be entering Bill's tunnel. It would be just a matter of minutes before he would be torn apart.

A weapon, thought Bill, I've got to have some kind of a weapon to defend myself with. Then it dawned on him that he was already holding a weapon in his hand. The pointed board! "Yes," he mumbled, "this'll do nicely. It'll make a good dagger, that is, if it doesn't break when I stab the animal. I've got to put together a quick plan of defense."

Staring at the burning pile of timbers, an idea suddenly came to him. Picking up the remaining six cartridges, he forced the tips into the crack in the wall. He managed to pull the tips free of the casings as he had done before. Tearing another piece of cloth from his shirt, he placed the powder into the piece of cloth, tied the cloth ends together, then placed the cloth sack into his jacket pocket.

The fire was still burning. The thought of putting burning embers in front of the small tunnel openings came to mind, but there wasn't enough wood left to make a big enough fire to scare both of the animals. Besides, Bill wanted his side of the tunnel dark when the animals clawed their way through the dirt walls. He might have a bit of luck in darkness.

Picking up the largest piece of burning ember, Bill kicked dirt onto the remaining pieces of burning wood, snuffing out the flames. He prayed that his plan would work as he made his way to the furthest corner in his part of the tunnel. The animals were almost inside of Bill's tunnel. He could hear the growls and snarls getting louder. Any moment, the animals would be in his part of the tunnel.

Sitting down on the ground, Bill placed the single burning ember in an upright position so that the flame would keep burning and not go out. Removing the cloth sack from his jacket pocket, he opened it and poured the powder on the ground approximately three feet in front of him. The powder formed a continuous semicircle around where he was sitting. He rested his head against the rock wall, closed his eyes, and waited.

The sound of a loud snarling *HISSSSSSSS* signaled Bill that it was time to open his eyes. The cougar was the first animal to enter Bill's part of the tunnel. He grabbed the pointed board, holding it tightly in his left hand, ready to protect himself from his attacker. Slowly, his injured hand moved towards the smoldering ember. He took hold of it. The flame had disappeared. Only a bright red glow covered the tip of the board as he brought it up to his eye level.

The cougar stopped, slowly surveying the contents of the tunnel. He didn't need any light to locate Bill Ross. The scent of Bill's blood was enough to find him. The cougar crept towards Bill - - one step at a time. Each step that he took was meant to terrorize his victim. He growled, snarled and showed his fangs. The thought of fresh meat made the cougar's mouth salivacate. Now was his turn! He was the hunter! He would kill the enemy that wanted him dead!

Dirt shot up into the air from the other side of the tunnel. Hans had broken through the mound of dirt. The first thing he spotted was Bill. He ran towards him, growling with anger and hate.

Bill Ross stuck the smoldering ember into the ground, guessing where the line of gunpowder was spread out. He covered his eyes and waited. Seconds later the gunpowder ignited. The tunnel quickly filled with a bright flash and an abundance of smoke.

Both Hans and the cougar stopped - - momentarily blinded by the bright flash. When Hans was able to regain his vision, he saw the cougar.

For that one short moment, Hans forgot about Bill and leaped at the cougar. The two animals rolled over and over on the ground, clenched tightly together, clawing and savagely biting each other.

Now's the time to make my move, thought Bill. I won't get a second chance! He quickly crawled across the dirt floor, pulling himself through the hole that the cougar had dug. The noise coming from the other tunnel was loud and vicious.

It's a fight to the death, thought Bill. With the last of his available strength, he dragged himself to the cave's entrance. The bright sunlight momentarily blinded him. Forcing himself up off of the ground, he slowly walked out to the open wilderness.

He only walked a short distance. His weakened condition forced him to fall down on the snow covered grass. A loud crash came from inside of the tunnel followed by a large cloud of dust that belched out of the cave's entrance. Moments later there was nothing but silence.

Bill guessed that both Hans and the cougar were dead. A single thought that kept running through his mind - - bothered him. Was Hans still loyal to his master when he saw the cougar and attacked him? Or, was Hans merely protecting his own meal from the cougar?

The crunching sounds of broken twigs came from the shrubbery below him.

"A search party," Bill mumbled as he lifted himself up off of the wet snow. He took one last long look at the cave's entrance before he went to meet his rescuers.

"I still believe that you were a loyal friend, Hans," he said softly, then turned and started down the mountain side to meet with his friends.

THE FORGOTTEN MEMORY

CHAPTER 1

The cold, sharp winds cut their way through the tall tree tops, freeing the remaining leaves still attached to the almost naked branches. It was late October. The season of autumn was almost concluded. The damp winds hinted of what was fast approaching.

An elderly woman sat in her living room in front of a large picture window, knitting, while she occasionally watched the falling leaves spin in circles, eventually reaching the ground. Her dark colored satin and lace dress hinted her to be a lady of refinement and wealth. The wearing of dark colored clothes always seemed to bring out the silverness of her hair. She looked much younger than her age of sixty-five. She was the perfect picture of one's sweet, old, maternal grandmother. Being the richest woman in Christian County, she was aloud to act strangely and do eccentric things.

Her husband had been missing for thirty years. Pronounced legally dead after seven years, the money, by law, from his estate and insurance was turned over to her. Each year the elderly woman would place an ad in the local newspaper. She had hoped that some day her husband would read the advertisement and contact her, providing of course, that he was still alive.

She picked up the telephone receiver, dialed a number and waited. A female voice at the other end of the line said, "Christian County Sentinel. May I help you?"

"Yes dear," the elderly woman replied softly, "may I have the ad department please?"

"One moment please," came the reply. A clicking sound repeated itself over and over. Finally, a rough, masculine voice barked, "*AD DEPARTMENT, CAN I HELP YOU?*"

"This is Mrs. Emily Constance Bradley speaking. I'd like to place the usual ad that I run this time each year."

"Yes Mrs. Bradley. I was going to call to see if you wanted to run your ad again this year. It's getting close to November 1. Did you receive any replies from last years ad?"

"No... nothing... as usual," she replied discouragedly.

"Do you want the ad to read the same as before, or do you want to make some changes?"

"No," she hesitated a moment, "print it the same as you always have in the past."

"Let me read it back to you Mrs. Bradley, just to make sure it's correct."

RALPH BRADLEY, PLEASE COME BACK HOME OR AT LEAST CONTACT ME. - I HAVE PLENTY OF MONEY TO SUPPORT US. - I NEED AND MISS YOU. I STILL LIVE AT THE SAME ADDRESS, -- 136 FLORTON DRIVE. - LOVE, EMILY

"Pardon me Mrs. Bradley, but aren't you afraid you'll get some dishonest people to bother you?" asked the ad man. "It's not the best practice to print your name and address in the ad."

"No," replied Emily Bradley, a little chuckle in her voice, "I've had a few calls through the years, but I knew they weren't from Ralph. I just ignored the callers. I'll know when Ralph gets in touch with me."

"How long is it now since Mr. Bradley's disappearance?"

"It'll be thirty years come this November 1st. That was the last time I saw and heard him speak to me."

"Shall I bill you the usual way for the ad?" asked the ad man.

"Yes, that will be fine. Good-bye and thank you," she answered.

"Good-bye Mrs. Bradley," replied the voice at the other end of the phone line. Hearing a click and the line going dead, Emily Bradley placed the receiver down on the phone's base and slowly rocked back and forth in her favorite rocking chair. She picked up her knitting bag off of the floor and began working on her knitting project.

The following morning the Sentinel ran the ad in the personal column of the newspaper. Emily Bradley went out on to the front porch, picked up the newspaper and walked slowly into her living room. She sat down in her rocking chair and put on her reading glasses. Thumbing slowly through the newspaper, she stopped at the section with the personal ads. Her right index finger slowly scanned up and down the long columns until she located her ad. She read the ad slowly, smiled, folded up the paper and set it down in her lap. Rocking back and forth, she began to knit. Occasionally she'd stop to gaze out of the living room picture window. Where are you Ralph? She thought. If only I could see you once more before I die. That's my only wish. Just to see you again before I die.

Several days passed with no response to the ad. Thursday came. The air outside was cold and crisp. An ancient relic, resembling a doorbell, echoed a weak but distinct call throughout the house. Emily Bradley searched through her kitchen cabinets, looking for something to make for lunch. Her thoughts concentrated solely on food. The doorbell gave its' call repeatedly. At last, it caught Emily Bradley's attention. She had so few visitors that it took awhile for her to recognize the strange sound.

She left the kitchen, walked down the long, dusty hallway and approached the front entrance door. Her thin, frail hand twisted the doorknob and pulled the door open, using a little of her reserve energy for the difficult task. It was some what of an ordeal for her to open the heavy solid oak door.

"Mrs. Emily Bradley?" said a middle aged man standing in the doorway, holding the screen door open. He wore a pair of coveralls covered with different colored swatches of paint. He spoke in a friendly manner as his face bore a pleasant smile.

"Yes, I'm Emily Bradley. What can I do for you?" she asked.

"My name is Gordon Gold. I'm a handyman and I'm new in town. I've been trying to get some clientele for my business. I plan on settling down in this part of the state. Some of the town folks told me that you lived alone and your home was badly in need of repairs, as I can see by this broken hinge on your screen door. I can fix anything and my prices are reasonable."

"Yes," she replied, giving the front of the house a quick glance, "my home is in need of some repair. Please come in Mr. Gold," she said as she turned.

"Thank you Mrs. Bradley," he replied, reverently tipping his hat as he entered the house behind her.

She lead him into the living room. They sat down and talked. Emily Bradley gave him instructions on what she wanted fixed. They both finally agreed on a price for his labor.

In the three days that followed, Gordon Gold repaired doors, steps and patched and painted walls. Besides doing the repairs, Gordon Gold did other tasks that the original job agreement did not call for. The extra duty tasks would be very beneficial for him in the very near future.

He searched the entire house... rummaging through everything. He searched every room, dresser drawer, closet and box that he could find. He searched not as a thief for valuables, but for information about the years that had passed. He looked for books, old letters, notes of any kind and photographs of two people that were very much in love so many years ago. He looked for those special moments in Emily Bradley's life. Gordon Gold had a plan - - a plan that would relieve all of Emily Bradley's earth gained wealth.

It wasn't until the fourth day of searching that Gordon Gold finally found exactly what he was looking for. In the attic, while doing some repairs to the roof, he came across an old trunk. Inside, he found old clothes, letters and photographs of Ralph and Emily Bradley. At the bottom of the trunk, Gordon Gold found the most valuable object of all - - Emily Bradley's diary. His plan could now be put into operation. He could forget the play acting of being a handyman and get down to the real reason he had come to Christian County.

II

The brake drums on the open backed truck screeched as it came to a full stop in front of Gordon Gold's temporary workshop. He got out of his truck and walked through the small entrance door at the side of the large wooden garage. Dick Lambert and Ronald Grubbs were seated at a small table in the north corner of the garage. Gordon Gold walked over to a small refrigerator, opened the door, removed a cold can of beer, opened it and took a long swallow. He let out a small belch as he walked over to the table and plopped himself down into an empty chair.

The two men watched him without uttering a single word. He took another long swallow and finished the rest of the beer that was in the can.

"Well," said Ronald Grubbs, throwing his playing cards down in the center of the table. His chubby fingers fumbled with an empty pack of cigarettes, looking for the last cigarette that he had already smoked.

Gordon Gold ignored Ronald Grubbs's question and asked one of his own.

"What game were you two playing when I came in?"

"Gin rummy," remarked Dick Lambert, readjusting his dark horn rimmed glasses that were resting on the bridge of his nose. "Cut out the damn dramatics and get to the point. Did you get the information from the old lady's house?"

Gordon Gold smiled, hesitated a moment, then reached in his shirt pocket. He took out a bundle of paper, bound together with a single rubber band and threw the bundle into the center of the table.

"There it is," he said, smiling. Dick Lambert reached for the bundle of papers. Gordon Gold continued speaking. "Everything that we'll need is right there in that bundle. Nobody could have pulled off this act better than I did. I grabbed that old ladies confidence right off from the start. I had no problem getting full run of her house. She trusted me implicitly."

"It took you long enough," said Ronald Grubbs, his fat cheeks vibrating like a bowl full of Jell-O every time he spoke. "We've been sitting here four days waiting for you!"

"So it took a couple of days longer than I had figured on. The extra time paid off! In a little while we'll all be rolling in dough," Gordon Gold shouted angrily, slamming his clutched fist on top of the table.

Dick Lambert remained silent. He rummaged through the photographs and papers that Gordon Gold had found. Using a small magnifying glass he removed from his pant's pocket, he closely examined the photographs, then looked up at Gordon gold.

"It won't be to difficult to get you to look like the old lady's husband, Gordon. Your facial features and his are quite similar. We've only got one real problem. How are we going to get you back into the old ladies house? You must have taken care of all the repairs needed in the four days that you worked there."

"Don't you worry," said Gordon Gold, smiling, "I've taken care of that small problem too!"

"What makes you so sure she'll call you back?" asked Ronald Grubbs, popping a gumdrop into his mouth.

"While the old lady was taking a nap, I took the back plate off of the refrigerator. I loosened the nut holding the pulley wheel on the motor shaft. Every time the motor starts and the shaft turns, the nut will loosen itself a little more until it finally falls off of the shaft. It shouldn't take longer than a day or two. While I'm there with her, I'll start the ball rolling. We became friendly and we talked a lot. It shouldn't be to hard to convince her."

III

Day one passed with no telephone call from Emily Bradley. On the afternoon of the second day, while the three men sat and played cards, the telephone rang. Gordon Gold set his cards down on the table, walked over to his desk and picked up the telephone.

"Gold's fix-it shop. Gordon Gold speaking."

"Mr. Gold," said a timid voice at the other end of the line, "this is Mrs. Emily Bradley. I seem to have a problem with my refrigerator. The motor constantly runs, but the refrigerator will not cool. Do you think that you might help me and possibly repair it?"

"Sure Mrs. Bradley. Don't you worry about it. It'll take me a little while to gather my tools and load them into my truck. I'll be there just as soon as I can."

Gordon Gold hung up the telephone. He looked over at the two men seated at the table. His face bore an *'I told you so '* look.

"Well boys, this is it! Just what we've been waiting for. That was old lady Bradley on the phone. Her refrigerator just broke down!"

IV

It was approaching 5:15 p.m. when Gordon Gold pulled up in front of Emily Bradley's house. He lifted his tool box out of the back of his truck, walked on to the front porch and rang the doorbell. He waited, then rang the doorbell several more times before Emily Bradley finally opened her front door.

"Mr. Gold, I'm so glad you finally arrived. I was afraid my food would spoil before you got here," she said, motioning for him to enter her house.

"Got here just as fast as I could Mrs. Bradley. A lot of traffic on the highway this time of the day. It shouldn't take me long to fix your refrigerator."

Gordon Gold walked into the kitchen and placed his tool box on the floor next to the refrigerator. He turned the refrigerator around so that he could remove the back plate.

"Why don't you go about your regular business Mrs. Bradley? I'll call you when I've finished."

Emily Bradley smiled and left the kitchen. Gordon Gold removed the back plate on the refrigerator, then lit up a cigarette. He had to kill a little time. He couldn't make the job look too easy or the old lady might get suspicious. Finally, he tightened the pulley wheel onto the motor shaft and reconnected the fan belt. A half hour had past. The refrigerator was running once again. The compartments were beginning to chill

Gordon Gold put his tools back into his tool box , then walked into the living room. Emily Bradley sat in her favorite rocking chair, slowly rocking back and forth, while she knitted.

"All fixed Mrs. Bradley. She's running good as new again. The pulley wheel just came loose, that's all it was. No big problem to fix."

Emily Bradley stopped knitting, looked up and smiled, "that's good Mr. Gold," she said. "I don't know what I would have done without your help. Would you please sit down and chat with me awhile? That is, if your not too busy."

"Sure Mrs. Bradley. I'm finished for the day anyway," he replied politely. "Are you married Mr. Gold?"

"Heck no!" he hesitated. "I'm not."

"Where do you eat all of your meals?"

"Sometimes I eat in restaurants. Other times I cook for myself."

"Mr. Gold, would you do an old lady a favor and give me the honor of having your company with me at supper tonight?"

Gordon Gold hesitated before answering. "Sure. I'd be glad to Mrs. Bradley," he finally said.

She cooked a simple meal for the two of them. They chatted a little while they ate. At the conclusion of the meal, they left the dining room and went back into the living room. Emily Bradley sat down in her favorite chair, while Gordon Gold rested himself in a large easy chair.

"Would you like a glass of sherry, Mr. Gold?" she asked. "It's good for warming up your bones on cold nights as these."

"Don't mind if I do," he replied contentedly.

"The sherry and empty glasses are in that cabinet in the corner," she said, pointing in the cabinet's direction.

Gordon Gold got up, walked over to the cabinet, picked up a bottle and two empty glasses and poured the sherry for Emily Bradley and himself. He handed her a full glass, then sat back down in the easy chair. She took a small sip of the sherry, then set the glass down on top of a small end table next to her chair.

"Do you mind if I continue to knit while we talk, Mr. Gold?" she asked. " I do enjoy my knitting. I don't get to many visitors ."

"That's O.K. with me Mrs. Bradley. Go right ahead and knit."

"You may smoke if you wish, Mr. Gold. My husband enjoyed a good cigar after his evening meal."

"Speaking of your husband Mrs. Bradley, while reading the newspaper this morning, I noticed your unusual ad in the personal columns of the paper. Has your husband been missing long"

"It will be thirty years come this November 1st. I run that same ad every year hoping that Mr. Bradley will read it and contact me."

"If you don't mind talking about it, Mrs. Bradley, I'd like to know some of the circumstances behind his disappearance?"

"It's really hard for me to remember after so many years, Mr. Gold. I do remember that it happened on November 1st. Mr. Bradley was leaving for somewhere and he kissed me good-bye. I never saw him after that."

"Did you call the police when he didn't come home?"

"Oh my, yes. Two detectives came to my home and talked with me. They filled out the usual forms. Oh, they were very thorough about everything, but the investigation never turned up an answer as to what happened to Mr. Bradley."

"Do you still think he's alive?" Gordon Gold continued his questioning.

"I don't know," she replied. "I only hope that he is. I just want to see him one more time before I die."

"I don't like to pry into your personal business, Mrs. Bradley, but have you ever thought about going to see a mystic to help you?"

"Oh dear me, yes," she laughed." I've gone to see quite a few mystics, but none of them were ever able to help me contact Mr. Bradley. None of them could furnish the right answers to convince me that I was talking with Mr. Bradley."

"I have a friend, Mrs. Bradley," Gordon Gold interrupted her, "who went to see this particular mystic. He said the mystic was able to bring my friends uncle's spirit back from the dead. The spirit furnished my friend with answers that helped him locate some missing bank books and stock securities that were hidden away. I'll tell you, Mrs. Bradley, it was just amazing the way my friend described everything for me. Now don't get me wrong, I'm not saying that you should go to see this mystic. I wouldn't know how to get in touch with him if you wanted me too. I'd have to first contact my friend . But," he paused, "one never knows. This mystic might be able to help you." Gordon Gold looked at his wrist watch. "Oh my gosh!" he said. "It's seven thirty already. I've got to be going. I have to pick up a check from my last client."

"Speaking of checks Mr. Gold, just how much do I owe you for repairing my refrigerator?"

"The delicious meal you cooked and served me," he smiled, "along with your pleasant company is payment enough for the little work that did."

"Nonsense. You have to earn a living and I insist that I pay you."

"O.K. Mrs. Bradley. You win. Just send me a check for whatever you think the repair job was worth, but I really must be going now."

V

9:30 p.m. Gordon Gold stopped the truck in front of the farm house at 2116 Courlton Road. His eyes examined each window of the house, looking for some sign of activity. The porch light went on just as the front door opened slowly. Ronald Grubbs stood in the doorway eating a ham and cheese sandwich. He fumbled with the screen door latch while holding the sandwich with his left hand and a bottle of beer in his right hand.

Gordon Gold walked along the small circular sidewalk, then stepped up onto the front porch. As he walked passed Ronald Grubbs, he heard him mumble a few passages, but paid no attention to him. One quick glimpse examined the enterance hallway and large living room.

The walls of the entrance hallway were decorated with long, black drapes. He was especially impressed with the large white printed signs of the Zodiac upon them. Gordon Gold walked into the living room. A thick, blood red, colored carpet covered the entire living room floor. In the center of the room stood a single table made of dark oak. Placed around the table were four wooden chairs. A large clear glass ball, resting on top of a black marble pedestal, decorated the center of the table. Cabinet type tables were in each corner of the room. Dark blue velvet drapes decorated the walls, hiding the windows and doors.

The drapes, hanging on the north wall fluttered as Dick Lambert walked out from behind them. He was clad in a black cloak and wore a black turban. Walking along, his fingers thumbed through the stack of papers that he carried. He stopped and looked up. Gordon Gold, standing in the doorway, caught his attention. Sarcastically, Dick Lambert asked, "Well, did you convince her about seeing a mystic?"

"Yea! I spoke with her," Gordon Gold answered. "I do believe she took the bait I laid out for her. We should be hearing from her in a few days. What are you reading?" he asked.

"It's a small script that I've written. I also have the diagrams for the layout and the master control panel."

"Wow! This set up must have set us back a pretty penny. What did all of this stuff cost us Dick?"

"Only two grand. The electrical supplies were the most expensive. You know Gordon, the return that we get from this venture will be well worth it! How long did you rent the house for?"

"We've got a years lease on it, but I only paid the bank this months rent. The lease is made out to a phony person. They won't be able to trace back to me with it. I've got to go back out to my truck and get my tools. I've still a lot of work to do. Got to finish setting up the electrical equipment as soon as possible."

VI

Dick Lambert continued studying his papers. Gordon Gold proceeded to lay wire and connect the electrical equipment. Ronald Grubbs went back to the kitchen for more food.

It was a simple con game that they were going to pull on the old lady. The name of the game was - - getting money from her. The plan was simple.

A small control panel was built into the arm of the mystic's chair. It was covered with a piece of material that concealed the control buttons. Audio speakers were placed into each of the cabinet tables. A miniature light bulb was placed in the marble pedestal to illuminate the glass ball. They drilled a small hole in the ceiling, just above the mystic's chair. At the far corner of the room, in back of the potential victim, a one inch square piece of ceiling was cut away. Chemically produced fog would be forced through a small tube, having the mist form just over the mystic's head. An image from a projector would be shown on the vapor mist through a hole in the ceiling. The motion of the mist would produce the illusion of movement.

Gordon Gold worked quickly in the basement, making the final hookups to a tape recorder. He mumbled to himself as he worked. "Yes my two dear friends, we have pulled many a deal together but this job will make us all rich, for awhile anyway. But, on the other hand, if the money didn't have to be split three ways, one man could be very rich for the rest of his life." He carefully removed twenty sticks of dynamite from the bottom of his tool box and placed them in a wooden trash barrel, just under the living room floor. Carefully connecting a primer cap to one of the dynamite sticks, he ran the electrical wire from the cap to a small black metal box. Gordon Gold planned on making the final connections to the tape recorder and dynamite on the night that Emily Bradley came to the farm house. He covered the dynamite sticks with scraps of paper so they wouldn't be found if anyone happened to wander down into the basement.

Dick Lambert was seated at the table, reading, when Gordon Gold came up from the basement.

"All set, Gordon?" he asked.

"Yea, everything's ready to go. Just got a little something here that I've added for our show. Here, let me show you." Gordon Gold pulled back the material covering the control panel on the arm of the chair, exposing several small buttons. He continued with his demonstration for Dick Lambert. Ronald Grubbs came into the living room to watch. He was nibbling on a peanut butter and jelly sandwich. "Everything's still the same, Dick, except for a new red button that I've added to the control panel."

"What's it do?" asked Dick Lambert, looking puzzled.

"It serves a dual purpose. If the equipment becomes over heated, it will automatically cut off the electricity so that we don't blow a main fuse. When we're finished with the seance, you'll press the red button twice and it will disconnect all of the electrical circuits. Now, let's go over our plan once more. When Mrs. Bradley calls, I'll make arrangements to pick her up and bring her here. I'll convince her to go into the house alone, while I wait out in the truck for her. After she enters the house, I'll sneak in through the back door. I'll get dressed and then go into my act. Have you got the papers giving me power of attorney to handle her estate?"

"Right here in my shirt pocket," said Dick Lambert, chuckling as he patted his chest with his hand. "They're notarized and signed by you as her executor. All they lacking is her signature!"

"Good. All I have to do is convince her that all she's signing is a pledge for a charitable organization, and, as her dead husband it's my wish that she do so! After she signs the papers, I'll leave the room, undress and I'll go back to my truck with the papers. You'll continue talking with her, giving me time to get back to the truck. There is one more important fact and it must be timed just right. You must not press that red button on the control panel until you hear me start up the truck and pull away. Leave the music playing after we leave. It's merely for effect, you understand. Well, that's it. Let's all hit the sack!"

VII

Emily Bradley called Gordon Gold, just as he had anticipated. It was exactly a week to the day, since their talk, when Gordon Gold and Emily Bradley pulled up in front of 2116 Courlton Road. At first, the farm house appeared to be deserted. The lazy falling snow had covered the ground. The moonlight gave a bluish tinge to the thin white blanket.

Emily Bradley exited the truck. Carrying her knitting bag, she walked up onto the front porch. She pressed the doorbell button and waited. After a few moments, the door opened. Dick Lambert stood in the entrance way dressed in his mystic costume.

"Mrs. Emily Constance Bradley?" he asked.

"Yes, I am," she replied.

"I am Exandor, the greatest of all mystics. Welcome to my home. Please follow me into my meditation chamber where the restless spirits from the unknown wander endlessly until they are summoned by me to appear."

Emily Bradley followed Dick Lambert into the living room. She sat down in a chair opposite him in the center of the room.

"How may I serve you, Mrs. Bradley?" he asked.

"I want to know if my husband is dead. He disappeared thirty years ago. I haven't heard from him in all that time. I would like to know if he is living or dead."

"If your husband's spirit walks among the other spirits of the unknown, I will summon him forth to appear here before us. But first Mrs. Bradley, you must truly believe in the spirits before we can beckon them to appear."

"Oh, I do believe Mr. Exandor. I truly believe in them!"

"Then Mrs. Bradley, let us begin."

Dick Lambert moved the cloth on the arm of the chair and pressed the first three buttons simultaneously. The lights went out - - Eerie sounding music began - - The clear glass ball acquired a bluish glow.

Emily Bradley chuckled to herself. She had been on this route before when she had gone to see the other mystics in the past. They all seemed to have the same type of technique. Dick Lambert pressed another button that started the chemical mist. A thin white vapor seeped out through the tiny tube and hovered over Dick Lambert's head. The projector switched on but did not flash an image onto the vapor mist.

"What was your husband's first name?" asked Dick Lambert.

"Ralph. It's Ralph ," she replied. Dick Lambert went into his act.

"Ralph...Ralph Bradley. I, Exandor the greatest mystic of all, summon thee from the deepest depths of the unknown. I order thee to appear here before us by all of the powers given to me through the secrets of Satan." Dick Lambert continued to mumble muffled tone phrases while Emily Bradley watched and remained silent.

Gordon Gold entered the house, using the back door, and went directly to the basement. He connected the wires from the detonator cap and the black metal box attached to the tape recorder. Picking up a microphone, he began reading his part from the preplanned script. An out of focus image from the projector flashed onto the vapor mist over Dick Lambert's head.

"Who summons the spirit of Ralph Bradley?" said Gordon Gold, using a disguised voice.

"Ralph? Ralph, is that you?" asked Emily Bradley.

"It is I. Who is it that summons me from my eternal rest?"

"It's me Ralph... Emily... your wife! I've had Exandor summon you to appear before us."

"What is it that you wish of me, Emily?" he asked.

"When did you die ,Ralph?" she asked." What happened to you?"

"It happened a long time ago, Emily. Five years to be exact. There was an automobile accident. The car that I was riding in was completely demolished. Emily, do you remember all of the good times that we had? That first summer when we were married. We spent most of our time at Palmers Beach resort. The fun we had, swimming in the lake and running through the hot sand with our bare feet. Do you remember the first day of our honeymoon? I tripped getting out of our car and sprained my ankle."

Gordon Gold mentioned places, dates and facts that only Emily Bradley and her husband would know. Emily Bradley became very nervous. She reached into her knitting bag and took out her knitting needles and ball of yarn. Unconsciously, she started knitting while she listened to Gordon Gold speak.

"Emily, do you remember the pet name that I gave you? It was... *PRECIOUS ONE.* "

Precious one? Thought Emily Bradley, that name is familiar. Memories from a dead past began to come alive. Memories that laid hidden deep in her subconscious began to fight their way through the long tunnel of her conscious mind. The little bits and pieces began to fall into place. Everything was coming back to her. She remembered!

It was early in the afternoon on Saturday, November 1. Today was her birthday. She had gotten back early from her shopping trip to town. Ralph wasn't supposed to be home yet. She decided to do some gardening in back of the house. She removed the dandelion weeds from her lawn, using a long metal dandelion puller.

After working on the lawn for several hours, she collected a cluster of flowers to put in a vase in the living room. She entered the house through the kitchen door. The sound of muffled voices came from the downstairs bedroom. Emily Bradley went to investigate. Quietly pushing the bedroom door open, she saw her husband and her sister in a passionate embrace while they lay on the bed. Ralph had called her sister his *PRECIOUS ONE* several times. Anger - - hate - - rage raced through Emily's body. Her hands trembled as she tightened them around the handle of the metal dandelion puller.

She tiptoed into the bedroom, listening to the secret lovers whispering softly. Standing behind her husband, she raised both of her hands above her head and brought them down swiftly. With all the strength that she possessed, she struck her husband in the center of his back. The murder weapon penetrated Ralph Bradley's body and stuck deep into her sister's heart.

Both bodies shook for a slight moment, then lay motionless. The sight of all the scattered blood had put Emily Bradley's mind into a state of shock. But, the will to survive was stronger. She disposed of both bodies, placing them in the deep hole of a three hundred year old uprooted tree, approximately one hundred feet in back of her house. She poured two bags of lime powder over the bodies and covered them with dirt. When she had finished, her mind had produced a mental bloc as to what had happened. Emily Bradley had truly believed that her husband had run away from her.

Emily Bradley's memory returned to her just as Gordon Gold made his entrance into the living room. He was clad in dark clothes. He had rubbed a phosphorus powder on different parts of his face so they would stand out under the projector's light.

Emily Bradley stood up when she saw Gordon Gold's image. She rushed towards him. Tripping over the chair leg, she fell towards the floor. Gordon Gold, forgetting himself, tried to catch her and break her fall. Emily Bradley's knitting needles found their mark deep in the middle of Gordon Gold's chest. He fell to floor screaming - - clutching at his chest.

Dick Lambert's fingers fumbled uncontrollably over the control panel frantically pressing all the buttons. He tried to find the button that would turn on the lights. His index finger found the special red button. He pressed it. The sound of thunder, a cloud of smoke and a huge fire ball consumed the house and all its' occupants, leaving nothing but a leveled piece of land with burning debris scattered everywhere.

MISTER HARDLUCK

CHAPTER I

The falling rain tapped a rhythmic tempo against the steam covered window in the dingy one room apartment. Loud thunderous explosions raced across the dark cloud covered sky. Harry Tidwell laid across his lumpy mattress, his head resting on a sweat stained pillow.

His eyes traced the zigzagging pattern of cracks in the dirty ceiling above him. Repeatedly, he tried to think of a way to occupy his time for the rest of the day.

Would it be the movies again - - or, perhaps just a walk in the park? Maybe a stroll along the lake front? What other exciting way was there to occupy his time? Questionable thoughts kept repeating themselves over and over again.

Thirty years old and he was still a bachelor. Harry's frail, thin body revealed that he wasn't eating any home cooked meals. The graying temples, his pencil striped mustache and long sideburns gave one the misrepresenting impression of distinguishment and success. Harry Tidwell was, with know doubt, the most misrepresented impression of a successful business man.

Working six days a week at the ribbon factory, he was forced to listen to the loud chatter of machinery all day long. After a time, the noise would drive any normal person crazy.

Here it was, Sunday, a day of rest and his head still ached from the chatter of the machinery. Cutting the large rolls of ribbon into smaller rolls and stacking them into cartons was one of his main job duties.

A new office receptionist had begun working in the main office of the factory. Millie Hampstead was her name. She was a fine looking specimen of a woman. Her long, blond hair clung to the tops of her shoulders. When she walked, her body swayed to a silent rhythmic beat. Her tight miniskirt looked as though it were a natural part of her body contour.

Harry had only spoken to her momentarily, but that was all that was needed. Harry Tidwell was in love! All of his life he really never could make his feelings know to anyone, mainly because, he really didn't know how to do it. All of his life, his ambitions had turned into total failure.

In grammar school the kids stole his toys, candy and lunches. High school was no different. He lost his potential girl friends to the other boys. In college, well, Harry didn't go to college. He had lost his scholarship to another classmate. Harry's life was just one big default after another. Not a penny saved in the bank, he couldn't let Millie know of his feelings. By the time he could save enough money, Millie would most probably already be married and have five children.

The rain had finally stopped. Harry looked at the alarm clock resting on top of his dresser. 5:45 p.m. Jumping off of the bed, he walked over to the chipped porcelain sink. He doused his face with cold water, trying to wipe away the drowsiness from his eyes. Slipping on his sport shirt and jacket, he left his apartment, went downstairs and walked out onto the wet sidewalk.

Not too bad for a walk tonight, he thought. Taking a few steps, he stopped, reached into his front pants pocket and took out what money that he had - - four dollars and seventy cents. Payday wasn't until next week. Yes, it was definitely going to be a walk tonight.

Harry tucked his hands into his front pants pockets, shrugged his shoulders and continued his walk. He admired the displays in the store windows, wishing that he could afford this and that. Once he even stopped at a hot-dog stand to get himself a tantalizing bite for supper.

His long stroll along the lake front was nice and every so often he'd stop and watch the young children playing in the wet sand.

Oh, to be young again and start all over, though Harry, I wouldn't make all the same mistakes. Oh well, he sighed, no sense in crying over spilled milk.

The daylight hours passed quickly. Harry wondered what the time was. He didn't have his wrist watch. It was back at its' temporary home, the *GOLDSTEIN BRASS BALL* pawn shop.

The ponies and cards had been rough on him this week. Of course, they had been rough on him the last fifty-one weeks too!

It wasn't long before Harry found himself walking through Kincade park. He counted the lines in the concrete as he walked along the semicircular sidewalks. He estimated that his walk had taken him approximately five miles.

His feet ached. A wooden park bench caught his eye and looked inviting. He sat down and relaxed. Lovers walked passed him, hand in hand, occasionally stealing a kiss. Drowsiness returned to his eyelids. It wasn't long before Harry was fast asleep.

II

A loud woman's scream woke Harry. He looked around. He was surprised that he had fallen asleep.

The park was deserted of people, except for a car parked next to the curb, a few feet away from where Harry was sitting. He watched the car's two occupants. Another scream came from within the car. It startled Harry. He got up from the park bench and ran behind a cluster of bushes - - directly behind the car.

Harry hesitated. Should he run over to the car and help the girl in trouble? He could try and bluff the guy? Maybe the guy would think that Harry was a cop! Anyway, his luck was bound to change.

Harry jumped out from behind the bushes and ran over to the car.

"Hey miss, having trouble?" he shouted. "Can I be of help?" Harry bent down and looked into the car, ready to start his acting career. His voice froze momentarily in his throat -- from shock.

"Mr...." he paused. "Mr. Coswell? What are you doing here?" he asked.

Alex Coswell, a man in his late fifties, looked as surprised as Harry. He was Harry's employer and owner of the ribbon factory.

"*TIDWELL - - HARRY TIDWELL?*" Alex Coswell screamed. "*WHAT IN THE HELL ARE YOU DOING HERE?*"

"W-W-W-Well sir, I was sitting on that bench, over there," said Harry, pointing, "when I heard this young lady scream." Harry looked at the pretty young brunette. An exciting looking girl in her early twenties. Her low cut, black satin dress revealed the reason Mr. Coswell had taken her out.

This wasn't Mrs. Coswell, thought Harry. He had met Mrs. Coswell at a Christmas party, at the ribbon factory, last year.

"*TIDWELL,*" Alex Coswell said sternly, "*I WANT TO SEE YOU IN MY OFFICE TOMORROW MORNING,*" he bellowed loudly.

Harry walked rapidly away from the car and out of the park.

Oh boy, now I've done it, he thought. There goes my job. I've done it again. I stuck my nose where it didn't belong.

III

The hotel sign blinked on and off - - *RED-WHITE-RED-WHITE.* Harry was upset. Even his supper began talking back to him. He flopped down into a large easy chair in the hotel lobby. The television set was on. It was the late movie. The conversation between two actors caught Harry's attention.

The movie involved a blackmailer. A smile enlightened Harry's face. He had found the solution to all of his problems. Blackmail! He would blackmail Mr. Coswell! After all, Coswell had so much money, he wouldn't miss a measly fifty thousand dollars. With all of that money, he could ask Millie to marry him.

Harry darted up the stairs, two steps at a time and ran to his apartment. What approach would he use on Mr. Coswell? These thoughts kept him awake all night long.

Should he come right to the point? Ask Alex Coswell for the money out right? Should he play it by ear? Should he listen to what Alex Coswell was going to say to him first, then spring the proposition on him?

Harry tried to imagine all the possibilities that the money could be used for. He laid across his bed and fell fast asleep - - dreaming.

IV

Early the following morning, Harry was awakened by the sound of a passing truck. He looked at his alarm clock. 9:15 a.m. Holy cow, he thought, I'm late for work.

Harry jumped out of bed. He was still dressed in the clothes that he had worn the night before. Quickly, he washed up and changed clothes. He looked into a mirror and momentarily stopped his rushing.

What am I rushing for? He thought. After our meeting this morning, I won't have a job if Coswell doesn't go for my proposition. Harry took his time getting to the ribbon factory.

The time clock's hands showed 11:00 a.m. when he arrived at the factory. Not bothering to change into his working clothes, Harry headed straight for Alex Coswell's office and walked in without being announced.

"Good morning, Alex," he said, giving a slight hand wave.

"*ALEX! WHY YOU...*," Alex Coswell fumbled over his choice of words.

"Now... now Alex...you just take it easy," said Harry.

"*TAKE IT EASY*," interrupted Alex Coswell. He continued, "you come late to work, barge into my office unannounced and start calling me by my first name. I still demand some respect around here."

"Now just take it easy," Harry continued, "I've thought about that little incident last night, and..., well I've decided to offer you a proposition, or...?"

"Or you'll do what Tidwell?" Alex Coswell interrupted again, "tell my wife?"

"Right Alex, and you know how nasty a divorce can get. The newspapers like a nice juicy scandal too."

"What's your proposition, Harry?" asked Alex Coswell.

"I've just a few simple requests, Alex. First, I want a new position with the firm."

"What kind of a position?"

"First, being in charge of the whole production line with full authority to do as I please."

"*WHAT*," shouted Alex Coswell

"Second," Harry continued, "I want a new office. One next to yours will do nicely. I want it furnished to my liking. Third, I want a salary of fifty thousand dollars a year."

"Why you're..., you're insane, Tidwell. What you ask is impossible."

"I have one further request, Alex," harry continued, "I want twenty-five thousand dollars in cash within three days."

"*WHAT*. Why I'll....." Alex Coswell was tongue tied for words.

"Go ahead, Alex, do what you want. Only remember that your wife will be pretty upset when she finds out about your little escapade last night. I've nothing to lose except my horse shit job, and believe me, that ain't much to lose."

Harry paraded back and forth in front of Alex Coswell's desk. He knew that he held the upper hand. At last, he'd found his game. He was going to be a winner!

Alex Coswell thought over the offer Harry made him. His face revealed the anger that he held within himself. "I'll have to convert some of my stocks into cash," he said. "I don't keep that kind of cash on hand."

"Do what you have to do, Alex, but have that money for me come Thursday morning. I assume the rest of my offer is accepted also?" he asked, smiling.

"O.K., Tidwell," answered Alex Coswell, "you've got me over a barrel."

"Harry..That's what you'll call me from now on... Understand?"
Harry laughed loudly as he approached the office door. He turned and looked back at Alex Coswell.

"Oh yes, Alex, just one more little thing. I'm taking the next three days off. I've some personal matters that need tending." Harry left Coswell's office. He finally approached Millie. He succeeded in getting a date for Saturday night. His luck had indeed changed. Everything was going his way for the very first time.

V

Three days passed. Harry was back at the factory, standing in Alex Coswell's office.

"I saw my office before I came in here, Alex," he said confidently. "I'm glad you picked out the furnishings that I suggested to your secretary over the phone.."

"Skip all of the bull shit, Harry. I want to speak with you only when it's necessary. Your office is ready. The payroll department has been notified of your promotion and your salary is now fifty thousand dollars a year. And here's the last part to our deal." Alex Coswell opened the center drawer of his desk. He reached in and took out a large brown manila envelope. He looked at Harry for a moment, then threw the envelope on top of his desk in front of Harry. "Here," he said, angrily.

Harry picked up the envelope and quickly tore it open. He looked inside. The sight of all of that money made his eyes open to the size of silver dollars. He dumped the contents of the envelope on top of the desk.

"Don't you trust me, Harry?" asked Alex Coswell, lighting up a cigar.

"Just checking, Alex," he replied. "Anyone can make a mistake you know."

Thirteen bundles of money lay on top of the desk. Twelve bundles each contained two thousand dollars of both new ten and twenty dollar bills and one bundle contained one thousand dollars in new twenty dollar bills.

"I'm glad you got it in small bills as I requested, Alex. It'll make it easier for me to spend."

"I did what you requested, Harry. Now I've kept my part of the bargain. Are you going to keep yours?" Coswell asked, puffing on his cigar.

"I've already forgotten about that incident, Alex. Completely wiped it out of my memory. You can trust my old boy."

Harry picked up all the bundles of money and put them back into the manila envelope. He tucked the envelope under his arm and started to leave the office. He turned and looked back at Alex Coswell.

"Oh, just one more thing, Alex. I'm taking the rest of the week off. Have to get a new apartment, clothes, a car...to go with my new position and image. You do understand, Alex? Don't you?"

"Yes, I understand," replied Alex Coswell, turning the back of his chair towards Harry.

VI

The days that followed were sure enjoyment for Harry. He spent money everywhere - - a new apartment - - a new car - - a complete new wardrobe. And finally, a diamond ring for Millie. A wedding ring!

Saturday had finally arrived. The clock on the fireplace mantle chimed 2:00 p.m. Tonight, Harry decided to pop the big question - - marriage.

He relaxed on his new couch, sipping a very dry martini while he watched television. The program he was watching was suddenly interrupted for a special news bulletin. The announcer said;

"Ladies and gentlemen, we interrupt this program to bring you a special news bulletin. Today, The FBI arrested people involved in a major counterfeiting ring that has been under surveillance for two years. The FBI raided the Coswell ribbon factory at 1811 East 9th Street. Arrested was a Mr. Alex Coswell, the owner of the ribbon factory.

As the leader of an international counterfeiting ring, Coswell used the ribbon factory as a front for his operations. Coswell specialized in making phony ten and twenty dollar bills. The bills, almost being perfect, were discovered with one small imperfection on them. The engraver left off one half of an ear on the president's portrait.

This is the only means of identification between the counterfeit and real money. We are now resuming our regular scheduled program."

Harry sat motionless, disbelieving what he had just heard. His eyes stared blankly at the television set, seeing nothing but the picture of the FBI agents leading Alex Coswell out of the ribbon factory and placing him into the back seat of a police car.

Harry set his drink down on top of the cocktail table. Leaping off of the couch, he rushed over to the closet, opened the door and took a brown manila envelope off of the top shelve. He went back to the couch and sat down. Dumping the contents of the envelope on top of the cocktail table, he rapidly thumbed through the ten and twenty dollar bills. All the president's portraits had half of an ear missing.

"COUNTERFEIT...IT'S ALL COUNTERFEIT!" he screamed. "I've been passing counterfeit money all over town. I left my name and address everywhere that I made a purchase."

The doorbell chimes rang twice, but Harry was too ingrossed with the money to hear it. A loud pounding on his entrance door startled him, but it caught his attention.

"HARRY, HARRY TIDWELL, "shouted a voice from the other side of the door, "OPEN UP...THIS IS THE POLICE... WE KNOW THAT YOU'RE IN THERE!"

Harry scooped up the money and shoved it back into the manila envelope. Beads of perspiration formed on his forehead. He suddenly felt sick. He wanted to vomit - - but he couldn't.

I've got to get away, he thought. He couldn't speak. For some reason, his mouth and throat had suddenly gone dry.

A heavy object suddenly slammed against the entrance door. Harry tucked the envelope under his arm. He ran to the window that was on the street side of his apartment. As he approached the window, he turned and looked towards the door, only to see it come crashing down. Two men entered his apartment

I've got to get away, thought Harry. He leaped out of the front window onto the fire escape - - that wasn't there.

Harry's screams drowned out all his thoughts as his body plunged towards the sidewalk below. Harry had forgotten that the fire escape was on the alley side of the building.

THE LAST BUBBLE

CHAPTER I

Barbara Bennett and Sandy Simpson waited on the corner of Glendale Avenue for the traffic lights to change colors. A new red colored Ford convertible came to a quick screeching stop in front of them.

"Hi girls," said Norman Codwell.

"Hi Norman," they both replied.

"When did you get the new car?" asked Barbara.

"It's another present from my dad. He's leaving town again. He called the auto dealer yesterday and told them to let me pick out whatever type of car I wanted. This is what caught my eye."

"It's sure a honey. Cost much?" asked Sandy.

"Twenty-five grand," said Norman, rubbing the top of the steering wheel with his hand.

Sandy walked seductively towards the new car. She rubbed her hand on the smooth finish, resting her slim petite body on the front fender. Her colorful checked poncho and tight toreador slacks blended with the car's color. Her small emerald green eyes, jet black hair, fixed into a pony tail, excited Norman

"I wish my father would give me a present like that," said Sandy.

Yea, thought Norman. Every time he has to go out of town for a long time, he leaves me home alone and always buys me a present to keep me happy. It's been like that ever since I was ten years old, when mom died.

Norman looked at Barbara. Her blond hair brightened with the help of the rays from the sun. Her blue eyes twinkled like crystals. The clothes she wore weren't flashy, and yet, her clothes revealed just enough to make the boys interested in what they saw.

"By the way, Sandy, my dad won't be using the cottage this weekend." Norman continued. "He has to fly to New York City...again. A show producer has decided to produce a play of dad's latest book. He wants dad to be there when actor's audition for parts in the play. We can have a party at the cottage this weekend."

"Great," replied Barbara enthusiastically.

"You furnish the girls," said Norman, "and I'll get the guys. We'll have a swell time. Oh, by the way, I've got a little surprise to show everyone when we get to the cottage."

Norman removed a pair of sun glasses from the glove compartment. He put them on. Looking into his rear view mirror, he retied the blue silk scarf wrapped around his neck. Nonchalantly, he unbuttoned the top button on his white sport shirt. Not bad, he thought to himself.

"Well girls, I'd better get going. Got a lot to do before the weekend comes." Putting the gear selector into the drive position, he sped up Glendale Avenue, resembling a speed boat skimming across the waters of a lake. The traffic lights changed colors and the two girls crossed the street.

"Who should we ask to come with us, Barbara?" asked Sandy.

"How about Laura Hansen, Debbie Witts and Christine Morley?"

"Let's give them a call now," said Sandy. The girls raced each other to Sandy's house.

Norman Codwell drove up his circular drive, stopping at the front door of his twenty-two room house. He turned off the car's ignition, then ran into the house.

"*DAD...OH DAD!*" he shouted. A folded piece of white paper, propped up against a blue flower vase, standing in the center of the entrance hall table, caught Norman's eye. He walked over to the table, picked up the paper and began to read:

Norman,
Had to leave sooner than I had expected. Trouble with the script.
Have to do a lot of changes. Will be gone a couple of months.
Have deposited a substantial amount in your checking account
to tide you over till I get back.
Father

Norman angrily crushed the note in his fist. Reads just like a damn telegram, he thought. Couldn't even sign the note...*DAD*. Always so damn formal about everything. He stormed into the kitchen looking for the housekeeper.

"*HILDA....HILDA!*" he screamed. "When you want that damn woman, she's never around. And when you don't want her, she's always at your side," he mumbled aloud.

He walked over to the refrigerator, opened the door, took out a cold can of beer, pulled off the metal tab and went into the den. He took a swallow of beer from the can, set the can down on top of the desk and picked up the telephone book. He sat down in the huge black leather covered chair behind the desk. Thumbing through the phone book, he found the telephone numbers of the people he wanted to invite to the party. Picking up the telephone, he placed his first call to Bob Wimms. The next calls went to Tom Felton, Mike Towbart and Bill Holister. After all his friends agreed to come to the party, he dialed Sandy's telephone number.

"Hello, Sandy?" he asked.

"Yes," came the reply.

"It's Norman Codwell."

"Yes Norman. What do you want?" she asked.

"Got the guys for the party Saturday night."

" And I've got all of the girls too," she replied.

"Great. Meet me at my house late Saturday afternoon. We'll all drive up together."

"Right. See you Saturday, Norman."

"So long, Sandy." He replied.

Norman hung up the phone, picked up the can of beer and took a long refreshing swallow.

I'd better order some things for the party, he thought. He dialed the number for the delicatessen store.

"Hello? Is this Morrie's delicatessen?' he asked, irritated by the voice on the other end of the telephone line. "This is Norman Codwell speaking. *NORMAN CODWELL!*" he shouted into the telephone. "Let me speak with Morrie." There was a moment of silence. Finally, a voice said, "Hello?"

"Who in the hell answered the phone, Morrie?" Norman listened a moment then continued speaking. "Well, you ought to tell your new help who your important customers are. Forget it, Morrie. Morrie, just forget it. I accept your apology. Got a pencil and paper handy? O.K., I want half a case of gin, half a case of good scotch and a full case of your best bourbon. I'll also need a case of your best champagne and six cases of ice cold beer. No, I won't pick them up. Send it all to my cottage. You've delivered there before. But first, stop here at the house on your way up and I'll give you the key for the place. Oh yea Morrie, I'll need some food too. Send me twenty-five pounds of mixed cooked meats. Anyway you like, Morrie, rare, well done, some medium, whatever! I'd also like five pounds of mixed cheese and ten pounds of mixed salads. I also want six large trays of chopped liver, lobster, shrimps and other delicacies that you might think of. Morrie, I don't care what everything will cost! Just put it on my dad's bill. I want everything delivered at four o'clock. We won't get up to the cottage until about 6:00 p.m."

Norman hung up the phone. What a character, he thought. Picking up the can of beer, he finished what was left. Leaping out of his chair, Norman walked back into the kitchen.

"HILDA... HILDA," he shouted again.

"God-damn that woman," he mumbled.

Norman stormed out through the front door of his house, got into his car, started it and drove off in the direction of MACS Bar & Grill for a bite to eat.

II

Saturday finally arrived. Norman was awakened by Hilda's voice. His breakfast was ready, hot and waiting for him. He slowly rolled out of bed, yawned, stretched his arms up into the air, then looked at the clock on top of the dresser - - 10:30a.m. He felt good. Tonight he'd be surrounded with company. He hated being alone. He washed, dressed, then raced down the staircase leading to the dining room.

"Good morning, Hilda" he said, smiling.

"Good morning Mr. Norman," she replied politely.

"Lovely day, isn't it?" he asked.

"Yes sir, it is."

Hilda went into the kitchen and immediately brought out Norman's breakfast on a silver tray. She placed the plates of food in front of him. He picked up the glass of cold orange juice and quickly drank it down.

"*Hummmmm*. These eggs sure smell good," he said after smelling their pleasant aroma. "Tonight's going to be a perfect night for having a party," he said to Hilda.

"Are you having another party, Mr. Norman?" she asked.

"Yes, up at the cottage. Why?"

"I don't think that your father would approve of......" Hilda's speech was cut short. Norman stood up, threw his napkin on the floor and stormed out of the dinning room.

"Mr. Norman, where are you going?" she asked, "what about your breakfast?"

"*OUT*," he shouted.

Norman walked quickly to his garage, opened the large overhead door, started his car and raced down his drive way. He didn't want to be home with Hilda, having to listen to her preaching to him all day long. She always complained about his parties and drinking.

Norman thought about his last party. One of his guests had complimented him. "Norman," he said, "you always throw one hell-of-a party!" That made Norman feel good. At least someone was complimenting him for doing something on his own.

3:45 p.m. Norman arrived back at his house. He was half way up the staircase when the door bell rang.

"*HILDA,*" he shouted, "*GET THE DOOR.*" There was no reply from the kitchen.

"*HILDA,*" he shouted again. "God-damn that woman," he mumbled to himself. He walked back down the staircase and opened the front door. "What do you want?" he said sarcastically to the stranger standing in the doorway.

"Are you Mr. Norman Codwell?" asked the stranger.

"Yes. Why?"

"I'm from Morries's Deli. The name's Jeff. I'm suppose to pick up a key and deliver these groceries to your cottage."

"Just a moment." Norman went into the den. He opened a drawer in the middle of an oak desk and removed a set of keys. "Here they are," he said, handing them to the delivery man. "By the way, is that beer good and cold?"

"Yes sir, it is," said the delivery man.

"What about the champagne?"

"You didn't say you wanted it chilled, but Morrie took the liberty of chilling it for you anyway."

"Good for him. Make sure you put everything in the refrigerator right away. I want everything to be chilled when we get there."

"Yes sir. What should I do with the keys when I'm finished?" asked the delivery man.

"Oh," Norman hesitated a second, "just leave them on the table. Set the door latch and slam the door shut behind you. I've another set of keys for the place."

The delivery man got into his truck and drove off in the direction of the cottage.

At five-thirty the doorbell rang again. This time Hilda answered the door.

"Mr. Norman," she called, "your friends are here to see you."

Norman Codwell came out of his bedroom and walked down the staircase. "He everyone," he greeted them, "ready for a weekend of fun?" he asked. They all were cheerful and ready to go.

"How many cars have we out front?" asked Norman.

"Two," Bill Holister replied.

"This is what we'll do," suggested Norman. "I'll drive my car. Sandy will ride with me. The other two cars can follow us." Norman couldn't take his eyes away from looking at Sandy.

They all agreed.

"What's the surprise you told us about this afternoon?" asked Sandy.
"You'll see it when we get there!" was Norman's answer.

III

It was 5:50 p.m. according to Norman's wrist watch when they pulled up in front of Norman's cottage. They parked the cars if front of the four stall garages. Bill Holister got out of his car and remarked, "Wow...a cottage he calls that place. It has to have at least ten bedrooms."

"What's that strange buzzing noise?" asked Sandy.

"Walk over to the pier and see for yourself," said Norman, smiling.

"Pier? What pier? You don't have a lake out there," said Sandy.

"That's my surprise, Sandy. Look, dad's having a man made lake put on the property."

"How big will it be?" asked Bill Holister.

"It's a mile wide and eighty feet deep at its deepest point. Dad bought up three square miles of property surrounding the cottage. The workers are just doing some finishing touches. Tomorrow they'll start filling it up."

"What time?" asked Bill.

"They've estimated around 4:30 a.m. That's what the man from the water reservoir said."

"What reservoir?" interrupted Sandy.

"The one at Markton City. Dad had a thirty-six inch pipe line laid in order to bring the water from the reservoir. It'll fill the lake in no time and it'll keep it supplied with fresh water all of the time. O.K., that's enough of that. Let's go into the cottage." Norman opened the front door. They followed him into the house.

"Will you take a look at this place," said Bill Holister. This was the first time he had seen the inside of the house. He whistled as his eyes examined the large rooms.

"Bill, get the food and refreshments from the kitchen!" said Norman as he slid his arm around Sandy's thin waist.

"No Norman, you be a honey and get them yourself," said Sandy, smiling. She softly patted Norman's cheek. "I've got some new records out in the car. You know how good Bill and I dance together. And right now, I feel like dancing."

Sandy slipped away from Norman's grasp and walked over to Bill Holister. She took hold of Bill's hand and they walked over to the phonograph to select some records to play.

Norman's face twitched with anger. Seeing the expressions on everyone's face told him that he had been made a fool. He couldn't hold an intelligent conversation when he was angry. His anger grew with intensity.

The music blared loudly from the phonograph speakers. Everyone paired off into partners. They began dancing. Norman stormed into the kitchen, slamming the door shut behind him. He made a fist and punched the wall in anger. Grabbing a bottle of bourbon, he ripped off the cap and filled an eight ounce glass. He gulped down half of the glass's amber liquid. Barbara Bennett came into the kitchen.

"Can I help you with anything, Norman?" she asked. Norman stared at her for a long time, then said, "Everything's in the refrigerator. Help yourself!"

Norman left the kitchen, ignoring Barbara's advances, still clutching the half filled glass and bottle of bourbon in his hands.

"HEY EVERYONE," he shouted, "listen up. Barbara's bringing out the food. Alcohol and beer is in the kitchen and at the corner bar, next to the fireplace. Help yourselves."

Norman sat down on the couch. He stared at Sandy and Bill, both having a good time. "Let's play a game of chug-a-lug," he said, speaking slurishly. Everyone gathered around him.

"You go first, Norman," said Sandy, kidding him along

Norman looked up angrily at Sandy...mad at her suggestion of him being the one to go first. He lifted the bottle of bourbon to his lips and began swallowing the amber liquid.

"Chug-a-lug... chug-a-lug... chug-a-lug," their voices began chanting slowly and softly - - then sped up and got louder. Norman finished the entire bottle of bourbon. Everyone cheered and clapped their hands.

The remainder of the night, Norman tried to be alone with Sandy. She kept giving him the excuse that she wanted to dance with Bill. He watched the two of them dance embracingly. You couldn't put a piece of thin paper between them when they danced the slow numbers. Bill kissed and nibbled at her neck and she obliged him by blowing air softly into his ear. They laughed. They kissed. They hugged. They did dirty dancing. Bill fondled her, exploring her private parts. She never resisted his advances.

Norman's drinking increased. He felt dizzy and nauseous. He suddenly made his way up to one of the upstairs bedrooms and passed out cold across the bed. Barbara Bennett found him an hour later. She went downstairs and told everyone that Norman was out for the rest of the night.

"Let's just call it a night," Sandy suggested.

"What about Norman?" asked Barbara, "he's in no condition to be left alone."

"I'll stay with him," volunteered Bill Holister. "I'll clean up. I want to have a few words with Norman anyway. Go ahead and go home." They all left.

IV

Bill Holister began cleaning up the untidy rooms. He suddenly stopped working. He felt dizzy. His feet became unstable. Staggering, he collapsed and hit his head on the corner of the stone fireplace. Landing on top of the metal fireplace shovel, blood oozed from the open wound over his right eye, onto the shovel and the floor. He laid still and silent.

It was 3:45 a.m. when Norman awoke from his drunken stupor. He listened. There was no sound of voices coming from downstairs. No music! The only sound that he heard was the clicking of the phonograph needle on the turning record table. He slowly lifted himself off of the bed. He felt nauseated again. The back of his head was pounding and the floor below his feet seemed to be moving back and forth. He staggered out of the bedroom. Grabbing hold of a wooden railing, he walked cautiously down the stairs.

His vision was blurry. Managing to find his way to the couch, he dropped down on top of it. He covered his face with both hands, trying to shake his mind clear of the cobwebs that had developed there while he was asleep. His vision slightly cleared.

Looking towards the fireplace, he saw Bill Holister lying on the floor. Getting up quickly off of the couch made him fall to his knees. He crawled over to the fireplace, placing his hands into a sticky substance. They felt wet. Bringing his hand closer to his face, he saw that the substance was red in color.

It was blood. *"MY GOD,"* he screamed, *"DID I DO THIS?* I can't remember. *I CAN'T REMEMBER ANYTHING."* He backed away from the gory scene before him. "I know that I was mad as hell at him, but mad enough to kill him? And yet, I must have. No one else is here." Norman tried to revive his memory as he tugged at Bill's motionless arm.

"Bill... Bill... for God's sake, please get up," he pleaded. Bill Holister didn't respond..

"He has to be dead," Norman mumbled aloud.

It was a strenuous struggle, but Norman managed to pick himself up off of the floor. He staggered into the bathroom, turned on the cold water in the tub and stuck his head under the miniature falling waterfall. He used a towel to wipe his face dry, then walked back into the living room. He stopped for a few moments and just stared a Bill Holister's motionless body.

I have to get rid of that body, he thought. I can't call the police. I can't remember if I killed him. What can I do with the body? Put him in my car and crash it into a tree? I could say that he stole the car and crashed while trying to get away. No, no one would believe that story. I could burn down the house with the body inside of it. No, that story wouldn't be believable either. I know, I could leave the body in the woods and hope for wild animals to tear it apart and drag it away. No, that idea wouldn't work either. I can't let this body be found. Everyone would think that I killed Bill because of last night... my damn jealousy. What I really need is a nice grave to bury him in.

That's it, thought Norman, I'll bury him at the bottom of the new lake. They haven't started filling it yet. No one will find his body there.

Norman located a working flashlight and went out into the garage. He selected a long piece of rope, a piece of tarpaulin, a shovel and a set of lifting weights to help keep the body down. He hauled everything back into the living room. Spreading the tarpaulin across the floor, he rolled Bill's body into the middle of it. He wrapped the tarpaulin around the body, securing it tightly with the rope, leaving an extra long piece hanging from the legs. He dragged Bill's body out onto the front porch, across the grass and onto the wooden pier. Turning on his flashlight, the beam of light guided his way to the other end of the twenty- foot long pier.

The flashlight's beam highlighted the landscape below him. Norman went back to Bill's body, took hold of the piece of rope wrapped around the legs and dragged the body over the piers planks. Reaching the end of the pier, he attached the metal weights to Bill's ankles. He rolled the body off of the end of the pier and waited for the thud. It seemed an eternity, but the sound finally came.

Staggering back to the opposite end of the pier, Norman picked up the shovel and slid down the side of the dirt embankment. His flashlight guided him over to where Bill's body lay. The digging task, for a final resting place for Bill, began.

Norman dragged the body into the shallow grave and covered it back up with the dirt that he had originally exhumed from the hole. Finishing his task, he crawled back up the side of the embankment. He felt relieved, now that the body was buried.

Back at the house, Norman cleaned the blood off of the fireplace, shovel and floor, destroying the evidence in the burning embers in the fireplace. Hypnotized by the flickering glow, Norman watched the flames slowly consume the towels with their hungry appetite. Completely exhausted from his trying task, he dropped down on the couch again and quickly fell asleep.

V

It was late in the afternoon when Norman was awakened by a tug at his arm. It was Sandy. She had come back to the house with the rest of the group. Sandy bore a terrified and worried look on her face.

"Sandy, what's the matter?" asked Norman. "What are you doing back here?"

"Have you seen Bill?" she asked. "Is he still here? His mother called us this afternoon. He hasn't been home. What could have happened to him?"

"I don't know where he is," replied Norman, "I haven't seen him since I passed out last night."

"He stayed after the party broke up," Barbara Bennett interrupted, "to clean up the house and then have a talk with you."

"Maybe he just got tired of waiting for me to get up and just left," said Norman . "Maybe he just decided to walk home? Maybe he's out in the woods somewhere? How should I know? What's his mother worried about anyway? Bill's a big boy. I'm sure he can take care of himself."

"That's just it," replied Sandy excitedly, "I found out something today about Bill that I never knew about before. Norman, did you know that Bill was susceptible to having dizzy spells?"

"Spells? What kind of spells?" he asked.

Sandy continued. "He blacks out, giving an illusion of being a dead person. His breathing gets very shallow and his pulse gets to be almost nonexistent. You can hardly hear or feel a heart beat. This is what his mother is worried about and wants us to look for him. She was calling the sheriff's office when we left. They should be up here anytime now."

"Sandy, did you say he only gives the appearance of being dead?" asked Norman, his words sounding choppy as he spoke

"Yes," she replied, starting to cry.

"*OH MY GOD ...NO,*" Norman screamed as he squeezed his temples with his hands.

Norman's face turned milky white in color. An expression of sickness dominated his normal facial expression.

"What's the matter, Norman?" cried Sandy. "What's wrong with you?"

Norman Codwell stood up. He stared towards the lake.

"*OH MY GOD ... OH MY GOD,*" he screamed as he ran out of the house and down to the edge of the pier.

Sandy followed close behind him. Norman fell to his knees, staring down at the spot where Bill Holister was buried. Norman didn't say a single word as he watched the water level of the lake rise over the shallow grave. Tiny air bubbles slowly rose to the water's surface.

"What's the matter, Norman?" asked Sandy. "There's just a few air bubbles down there, that's all."

Norman began to both laugh and cry as he watched the last of the small air bubbles rise to the water's surface - - burst - - then disappear.

FRATERNALLY YOURS

CHAPTER I

The large bell in the main corridor gave a signal. Classes for the day were over for the students at *Hancerst College*. Today was Halloween. A night of fun and festivities awaited for most of the students, except for those from the fraternity house of *PI-DELTA-EPSILON*. This was the special night for their fraternity initiation called *HELL NIGHT*. This year had four new prospective members waiting to join the ranks of the most popular campus people. The most popular frat house on the college campus invited only the most selective of people to join.

The prospective new members entered the frat house at exactly 6:30 p.m. They entered the building marching in single file. The first person to enter was Harold Witcomb. He was a shy, timid boy who was the grandson of Charles Hancerst, the college's namesake and founder. He was followed by Horace Bennett, basically a studious person. Horace had good manners and was a connoisseur of excellent clothes. His father was the owner of the largest engineering firm in Central City. Lawrence Malone strolled in behind them -- his hands inside of his front pants pockets. Care free and easy going, his only interest for attending college was to have a good time. His only reason for joining the fraternity house was that his father insisted upon it.

The last member to enter the house was Donald T. Stone. A typical type outdoor person, rough and tough. He feared nothing and no one. He also made it a point to make this fact well known. Most times, the other students thought that he was a bit obnoxious.

The four candidates were ushered into a large room on the 1st floor of the frat house. They were seated in chairs placed around a large oak circular table. Three members of the initiation committee were already seated at the table, waiting for them. No one spoke a single word. An aged grandfather's clock rested on the floor of the library, slowly ticking the seconds away.

"Gentlemen, please give us your undivided attention," began Robert Webb, chairman and spokesman for the committee. "As you know, for years we have held the traditional type initiation that our predecessors had designed. This year," he paused," the other members of the committee, as well as I, have decided on changing the initiation procedure." Everyone listened attentively. "I'm sure that you all are familiar with the Pennyfast Estate. That's where your initiation is going to be held tonight. You are all to stay in the Pennyfast mansion from 8:00 p.m. tonight until 6:00 a.m. tomorrow morning. That's when we'll come to let you out of the house. You're not to leave the mansion for any reason - - at any time - - or under any circumstances. Is that understood by everyone?"

All the candidates answered, "Yes."

"Are there any questions before we leave?" asked Robert Webb.

Harold Witcomb raised his hand and spoke. "Isn't there some kind of a story going around about the Pennyfast mansion being haunted?"

"Yes," replied Robert Webb, "there's a story circulating about the mansion, but that's just a myth. Only a stupid rumor believed by idiots who want to be frightened. I'll try to be brief. The house is located approximately a mile and a half out of town. Edward C. Pennyfast was a sinister and evil old man. He had regained, over a long period of years, most of the fortune that he had lost in the stock market crash of twenty-nine. Since that incident, he never trusted banks. He had his mansion converted into a sealed, self-contained vault. He had all of the windows lined with one inch steel bars, spaced five inches apart. The doors are made of solid steel and covered with a thin layer of wood for appearance sake."

"The opening and closing of the doors is controlled by a special device that makes it impossible to open the doors, once they are closed. Every room was equipped with a special release switch that opens the doors for an emergency situation. The only catch was that old man Pennyfast was the only person who knew where the switches were hidden."

"What about the guys that installed the switches," said Donald Stone, "they knew the secret."

"The three installers died three days after they finished the job. It's still a mystery as to who killed them." Robert Webb continued. "About 100 yards from the main house, Pennyfast had a mausoleum built. It's said that he had all of his dead relatives placed in there. This is where he wanted to be placed when he died. About two years ago he got his wish.

"It's a known fact that Pennyfast hid all of his money somewhere on the property. He swore when he died that he would always be around to look after his money. Oh, many people looked for it after he died, but no one ever found the secret hiding place. The disposition of the estate still isn't settled. The relatives are fighting over the property in probate court. That's why no one lives there today."

"Come on, Webb, you don't believe any of that bull-shit about ghosts and haunted houses, do you?" asked Donald stone, a smirk on his lips.

"Are there any more questions before we leave?" asked Robert Webb, totally ignoring Donald Stone's question. Everyone remained silent. "Fine. We'd better leave. It's a quarter past seven and it'll take us a little while to get to the mansion." They all left the fraternity house.

CHAPTER II

7:45 p.m. Several cars traveled slowly along the dusty, narrow road leading to Pennyfast mansion. Grotesque architectural outlines of the mansion stood out as a silhouette against the dimly, moonlit sky. As dark clouds passed overhead, an occasional beam of moonlight glanced off of the mansion's dusty windows.

The cars stopped in front of the main door leading into the mansion. All the occupants exited from the autos.

"Well, is everyone ready?" asked Robert Webb. "It's almost 8:00."

Everyone replied, "Yes."

"I'll remind you all just one more time, "continued Robert Webb , "you are not to leave the inside of this house for any reason. No one is to have any objects with them other than the clothes on his back. If you do, give us what you have right now."

No one made any gestures to give anything away.

"O.K. gentlemen, let's go inside. We'll make sure that you're locked in nice and tight," said Robert Webb, smiling.

The candidates walked up the steps, leading to the front porch,and through the front door which had already been opened by one of the boys on the committee.

The door slammed shut behind them. Everyone remained silent and motionless, listening to the footsteps walking down the porch steps, the sound of the car motors starting and the autos pulling away from the house. Donald Stone tried the doorknob.

"Well, I guess we're on our own," he said, chuckling. "Let's look around and see what this place really looks like."

Strong winds howled through the open holes in the roof that had been left there by the previous winters. The mansion displayed all the visual signs of not being attended too for many, many years. A thick layer of dust covered everything. Giant spider webs connected the ceilings to the walls. The air was stale and stagnant from the lack of fresh ventilation. There was a mysterious uneasiness about the room. The candidates were a little concerned about the long hours of darkness awaiting them.

"Come on you guys, cheer up," said Donald Stone, "let's look around. We'll start in this room."

They walked into a darkened room. It was the study. Donald Stone reached into his front pants pocket and removed a small penlight flashlight.

"Hey," said Horace, "what are you doing with that? You know we're not suppose to have anything like that with us."

"Aw shit. Stop your fuckin bitchin,'" snapped Donald Stone, "I forgot that I had this. Anyway, we can use it. Say, will you take a good look at this room. It really must have been some room in its day."

Donald Stone slowly moved the flashlight beam around the room. He stopped it on a picture that was hanging over the stone fireplace. "Holy shit, will you look at that," he said. "All those wrinkles in one single face. What a horrible looking mug. Who do you think he is ?"

"Probably old man Pennyfast himself," Horace answered.

"A face like that belongs buried underground," said Donald Stone, laughing as he spoke.

The sound of heavy footsteps walking across the floor above them attracted their attention. They ran up the wooden staircase leading to the second floor landing.

"Where do you suppose those footsteps came from?" asked Larry.

"This room, I think," said Harold, walking towards the wooden door.

"Gee, I hope this night passes quickly."

"Don't worry Horace, it will," interrupted Donald Stone, "we'll keep busy tonight. Here, let's try the door." He slowly turned the doorknob and forced the door open. He illuminated the room with his flashlight's beam. They surmised that it was the master bedroom.

The door suddenly slammed shut behind them. Everyone turned around. A quick check of the room's occupants revealed that everyone was still in there.

"Never mind the door," remarked Horace, nervously, "come over here to the window."

"What is it?" asked Donald Stone.

Horace continued. "What's in that building in back of that clump of trees?" he asked.

"I would say that's the mausoleum that Robert Webb was telling us about," said Donald.

"Try the door. Let's get out of here, this room gives me the creeps," said Larry, anxious to leave.

Donald Stone reached for the doorknob. It began to turn by itself. Right to left. Left to right. No one else noticed the movement. He quickly took hold of the doorknob. Twisting and pulling it did no good. It wouldn't budge.

"Let me try it," said Horace, walking towards the door. He gave the doorknob a quick twist to the left. The door opened. "See, nothing to it when you know how." He laughed.

Horace stepped out into the dark corridor. The door slammed shut behind him. During the following two minutes, the most hideous scream of fright that they have ever heard echoed throughout the house. Then it suddenly stopped. No more screams. No movement of any kind could be heard. No trace of Horace. Only silence came from beyond the door. Harold pounded on the door.

"Horace... Horace!" he shouted. "Answer me. Are you O.K.?" There was no reply.

"Try the doorknob again, Larry," Donald ordered.

Larry did. This time the doorknob turned. Larry pushed the door open. They all rushed out into the darkened corridor.

"*HORACE...HORACE!*" Donald shouted.

"Where do you think he could have gone?" asked Larry

"I don't know," replied Donald. "Maybe he got frightened and ran downstairs. I don't know where the fuck he is."

"Yes, that's probably where he went," Larry answered, willing to accept Donald's explanation. " Let's go downstairs and look for him." Larry ran to the opposite end of the corridor.

"Hold on Larry ... wait a minute," yelled Donald.

Harold took hold of Donald's arm. " Should we start looking for him in the rooms on this floor?" he asked.

"Maybe we'd better," agreed Donald. "Horace might be hiding in one of them."

Larry reached the door at the furthest end of the corridor.

"Wait... Larry... wait," called Donald.

Larry ignored Donald Stone's warning. He opened the door and entered the room.

"*Horaceeeeeee,*" he shouted. His concerned plea turned into a horrible scream. Harold and Donald ran to the room. Larry was gone. There wasn't a sign anywhere that he ever even existed.

"Larry ... God-damn it, answer us. Larry!"

"Take it easy, Harold," said Donald, "take hold of yourself. Come on, let's try and find a way out of this place. I've had enough of this bull-shit."

Donald Stone grabbed Harold's arm and led him down the corridor, down the staircase and into the dark dismal living room.

"What time is it, Don?"

"Five minutes to twelve. Why?"

"I just...," Harold's speech was cut short by the interruption of a loud moan that broke the silence engulfing the entire house.

"What was that?" he asked.

"I don't...," Donald was interrupted by the moaning sound.

"Could that be Larry, or maybe even Horace?" said Harold. "Maybe they're hurt and need some help?"

"I don't think so," replied Donald. "I don't think so," he repeated. A noticeable quiver was developing in Donald Stone's speech. Harold picked up on this almost immediately. It made the fear within him grow.

"What's the matter, Don?" he asked.

"Nothing...*NOTHING*," shouted Donald, walking around the room in a circle.

Strange noises were starting again. No moans, only the sounds of chains being dragged across the hallway floor.

Harold ran to the hallway. "Don," he said," My God," he paused, "there's no one here. Come...." Harold's speech was cut by the sound of uncanny laughter. It started as a low tremor and built into a great crescendo. Harold began to lose his composure.

"Harold... Harold," said Donald, trying to attract his attention, "listen to me. Together, we have to find a way out of here. You start searching this room. I'll examine the study. We've got to locate one of those release switches."

Harold nodded his head in approval without saying a word. Donald Stone went into the study. He could hear Harold's movements in the other room. Donald tried desperately to locate one of the release switches. He yanked dusty books off of the book shelves, throwing them on the floor. He tore apart furniture.

Then, for no reason, something told him to remain still. He listened. There were no sounds of any kind coming from the next room. Silence prevailed. A shuttering fear suddenly over came Donald Stone. Was he alone in the house? He ran to the living room. Harold was gone. Where was he? What happened to him? What had happened to all the others? Who was in the house with him?

Questions. Lots of questions started spinning around in his head. Beads of perspiration began developing on his forehead. He walked over to the stone fireplace - - then stopped.

His flashlight slipped out of his hand and hit the floor. Bending down to pick it up, he noticed something hanging from inside of the chimney in the fireplace. He reached up, grabbed the object, and yanked. The object fell out of the chimney, along with a pound of soot. Donald Stone soon realized he was holding a human arm in his own hands.

He ran from room to room, clutching the human arm to his chest, frantically calling out, "Larry...Horace... Harold! Where the hell are you guys? Somebody please answer me!"

CHAPTER III

3:30 a.m. Six persons sat in wooden chairs surrounding a wooden table in the meeting room of the fraternity house. Around one side of the table sat Robert Webb and two members of the initiation committee. On the other side of the table sat Harold Witcomb, Larry Malone and Horace Bennett. Robert Webb was laughing hysterically. His eyes filled with tears.

"I wish you guys could have seen the expressions on your faces," he said. " They were worth a million dollars."

"Yea, I bet they were," replied Harold, "I never want to go through anything like that again. Not for anything in the world."

"Will you answer a few questions for us, Bob?" asked Larry.

"Sure, shoot," he replied.

"Well, first of all, who was that walking on the second floor when we first got there?"

"That was one of the committee members getting things ready for the nights festivities."

"How did you manage to get the doors to close by themselves?" asked Harold.

"Simple. Are you familiar with the way radio control works?"

"Yea, I know a little bit about it," replied Larry.

"Well, we rigged a small receiver and actuator attached to a small motor and pulley. We placed it behind the lock on the inside of the door latch. We controlled the door by sending electrical impulses to the receiver to release and lock the door."

"How did you concoct my fiasco?" asked Larry.

"Aw, that was simple too. There's a trap door, in front of the door, just as you enter the room. We used the same technique on the trap door that we used on the bedroom door. We sent an electrical impulse and released the latch. You fell into a pile of foam rubber on the floor below. Just like Horace fainted in the corridor outside of the bedroom when the door slammed shut behind him, you passed out on your way down to the stack of foam rubber."

"How did you know when I was standing on the trap door?"

"We were watching you."

"But," Larry interrupted, "we heard you guys get into the cars and pull away. Besides, the house was locked up tighter than a drum. How did you get back into the house?"

Robert Webb laughed again before he spoke. "We didn't go back to the fraternity house. Tom and Mike drove the cars a short distance down the road and left them there. We entered the house by way of the mausoleum."

"Through the what?" exclaimed Harold.

"The mausoleum," Robert Webb repeated, then continued speaking. "You see, when old man Pennyfast had the mausoleum built, he also constructed a secret tunnel that lead from the mausoleum back into the basement of the house. There's a fake coffin built into the south wall of the mausoleum. You have to press down on the brass rail on the side of the coffin. One side of the coffin drops open. Pennyfast had it designed that way just as a precaution. If the house ever caught fire and none of the release switches worked, he'd have another way of getting out of the house."

"Pretty shrewd of the old man," said Harold, "But what about the chains and all of those other strange noises?" he asked.

"We prerecorded all of the stuff that we wanted on a portable tape recorder, then played the tapes back through the heating ducks in the house. The sounds carried through beautifully. I will admit one thing, it did sound a wee-bit scary."

"What about Donald Stone?" asked Larry. "When are we going to get him?"

"We'll leave him in the house till 6:00 a.m." Robert Webb hesitated a moment. "We'll get him and explain everything to him too."

"Why were we selected to be taken out of the house, Bob," asked Larry. "Why not Don too?"

"We didn't formulate as to who would go and who would stay," explained Robert Webb. "The one's who fell into our traps were the people we took out of the picture. It was as simple as that. Don just happened to be the lucky one to be left behind. By the way Harold, you were the easiest to get out of the house. When you were searching the living room, we put a little chloroform on some cotton, crept up behind you and well... here you are.

"Oh, incidentally, we had one more big hell of a surprise for one of you, but no one found it. We went to the morgue last night and stole a cadavers arm. The poor guy was in a train wreck that left him in pieces. Anyway, we stuck the arm up the chimney in the fireplace. I would have loved to see the expression on the face of the guy that had found it."

CHAPTER IV

5:30 a.m. The men had finished talking about the nights festivities. They left the fraternity house and drove off in the direction of Pennyfast mansion.

The winds had gotten stronger and the air colder. A thin layer of frost covered the top of the grass - - resembling a sheet of crystal.

It was 5:55 a.m. when their cars stopped at the front door of Pennyfast mansion. The cars' occupants exited and walked up onto the front porch.

"Look," exclaimed Harold, pointing towards the front door, "it's open."

"Don, are you in there?" Robert Webb called out. His voice echoed throughout the empty house. No reply came back from Donald Stone.

The men decided to split up, each taking a different direction to search for Donald Stone. Minutes later, they were all back in the living room.

"Did anyone find Don," asked Robert Webb.

No one had located any trace of Donald Stone.

"Let's check out the grounds," suggested Larry. "He's got to be out there somewhere."

The sun shot little rays of sunlight over the land as it rose from the horizon.

"Horace...Larry... Bob! Come out to the front porch," shouted Harold. They beckoned to Harold's call. "What's the matter? What did you find?" they all inquired.

"Look," he answered, pointing with his index finger.

A path of ruffled grass broke the pattern of the crystal sheet that covered it. The path lead to the mausoleum.

"Do you think he went in there?" asked Larry.

"Could be," replied Robert, "let's just go and find out." They ran to the mausoleum.

"Look, the door's open, "said Larry, opening it a little wider. "And there's wet footprints going inside."

"Quite fooling around and just go inside and see if he's in there," said Robert.

"Wait...listen. I think I heard something," exclaimed Harold.

A muttering sound, resembling weird laughter, came from within the darkened mausoleum.

"He must be in there," exclaimed Horace.

Slowly they entered the mausoleum, one by one. The rays of the rising sun slowly illuminated the interior of the mausoleum. In the corner, huddled close to the wall was the darkened silhouette of a person. The weird laughter continued.

The stone lid covering the coffin in the center of the mausoleum had been moved. The coffin inside had been opened.

"Don, is that you? Are you O.K.?" asked Robert Webb.

The dark silhouette moved slightly, but gave no reply. The men moved in closer for a better look. The sunlight had now illuminated the entire inside of the mausoleum. The sight before them left them speechless. The figure of a person stood up and moved towards them.

Behind the figure, on the floor, laid several stones from the brick wall along with several piles of shriveled up bills.

"*LOOK... MONEY!*" shouted Robert Webb.

Larry looked at the body inside of the coffin. He screamed. "*BOB...LOOK INSIDE OF THE COFFIN...IT'S DON!*"

Donald Stone's body laid motionless inside of the coffin. His face was the color of ashen gray. His arms tightly clutched the severed arm that he had found in the fireplace chimney.

The approaching figure held a metal opened box in its' arms. Several bills drooped over the sides and dropped to the floor with each step that it took. The figure's face was now clearly visible to them. Pieces of rotting flesh revealed parts of darkened bone from the cheeks and forehead. The hair was white, stringy and shoulder length. Its clothes were of the funeral style - - dirty - - unraveling, giving off a pungent odor.

"*IT'S OLD MAN PENNYFAST,*" screamed Robert Webb.

Cries of horror filled the mausoleum as the only escape door closed shut behind them.

SHORT PRAYER FOR A STRANGER

CHAPTER I

It's not what I wanted, thought Joel Melenka, it's what they gave me. He had just crossed the state line - - leaving Idaho - - entering Montana.

Three months prior, the city fathers, where he lived and had worked all his life, had passed legislation that made it a mandatory retirement for all police and fire personnel who had attained the age of fifty-five. Joel Melenka had just turned fifty-five the day after that legislation was passed.

Thank God the kids were all grown up, thought Joel as he drove along in his 1987 Oldsmobile Station Wagon. As a widower, after his children were already grown, he was glad the kids were on their way to successful careers. His daughter was modeling. Her photograph was on the covers of many famous magazines. His oldest son was doing a musical tour, playing loud raunchy music for crowds of screaming kids. His youngest son had married and had three lovely daughters. Both he and his wife were doing acting commercials for product advertisements. A movie career looked promising for the both of them. Yes, it was great to have the kids settled.

Joel Melenka had been born into city life where he lived until the day of his retirement. Now, he wanted to get away from all the steel and concrete. He hadn't really decided on living by a lake with a forest, or somewhere up in the mountains. He had set out on his search two months ago, traveling around the different states, looking to accomplish his quest.

His nephew, Steve, had moved into his house, to take care of it and the dog named Homer. He'd agreed to stay there until Joel had decided on just what he wanted to do with the house and Homer. Joel *would know* the exact place he wanted to live when it popped up in front of his eyes. Until then, he'd drive and wander around the country.

During his several months of traveling, Joel had met an enormous amount of people and made numerous friends. He admired the scenery, while living out of motel rooms. Each town he visited was more beautiful than the last - - as was each state.

The highway traveling took Joel to Tucson, Arizona to visit an old school friend. He spent a few days visiting with the friend, but was soon on his way again. Tucson was a large city and he wanted out from living with the steel and concrete.

In the early 1900's, Joel's wife's grandfather had homesteaded a piece of land in Lemon, South Dakota. The property size totaled one hundred sixty acres. Through the years, the property was passed on from one relative to another. It was said that a coal mine existed on the property, but was not being worked. When Joel's wife passed away, the ranch and property in South Dakota reverted to him.

His travels took him to visit the ranch. He was amazed at the size of it. It was much too big for him. He turned the property over to a realty agency to rent out and collect the monthly rents for him. Joel decided that it would be a good investment for him.

Joel Melenka was somewhat of a religious man, although, he wasn't very strict about going to mass on Sundays. Oh, he was ashamed for some of the stunts that he had pulled in his past, but it was nothing that he couldn't live with.

He did have one good religious trait. Every time he passed a funeral procession or if one passed him by while he was walking or driving, he would stop, take off his hat and say a short prayer for the stranger. Joel always figured that maybe the stranger only needed one more prayer to get him into heaven. He had hoped that his prayer was that one.

Driving along Interstate 15, he had just left the state of Idaho and entered Montana. Joel had started out driving early in the morning, only stopping once for a quick bite of lunch. He decided to miss supper. He wanted to see just how many miles he could cover that day. Anyway, when he stopped at a motel, he'd get a quick bite to eat somewhere. An open all-night cafe was always found near the motels.

The scenery along Interstate 15 was beautiful. Colorful Ponderosa Pine, Larch and Douglas Fir trees, along with various kinds of shrubbery, lined both sides of the highway. The sun was setting for the day. It's last rays of light shot through the tree branches like arrows flying through the air from an Indian attack.

Joel adjusted the sun visor above him to keep the rays of light out of his eyes. A female deer and two of her doe's ran across the road in front of Joel's car. He quickly maneuvered the steering wheel, narrowly missing the three road challengers.

He slowed down his speed. The incident had momentarily shakened him. Got to slow down, he thought. Might have other critters pull the same stunt on me down the road. He lit up a cigarette and silently laughed to himself.

It was now dark out. The car's headlights illuminated the highway as the miles added up on the speedometer counter. Joel looked at his watch - -

9:30 p.m. He mentally totaled up the hours he had been driving - - fifteen hours to be exact. He decided to find a motel in the next town that he approached.

Joel had just traveled over a wooden bridge that spanned across a small river. He shortly approached a hill with a steep upgrade before him. As he approached the top of the hill, his automobile's electrical system gave him a slight problem. The headlights and dashlights flickered several times, then the entire lighting system went out. Total darkness engulfed the entire area. Heavy dark clouds covered the entire sky, blocking out the moon's bright light.

Joel passed over the top of the hill doing sixty-five miles per hour. He banged on the dashboard with his fist. The lights flickered, then suddenly came on again. The headlights illuminated the road once again.

To Joel's sudden surprise, at the bottom of the hill, a car and house trailer sat in the middle of the road, blocking both the North and South lanes of traffic. Neither vehicle displayed any warning or hazard lights. The driver was drunk. He parked his vehicles, shut off the car's motor and lights and went to sleep.

Joel quickly turned the steering wheel, steering to the left, trying to avoid the waiting danger created by the parked vehicles in the middle of the road. His excessive speed forced him into some dangerous maneuvers. The automobile's front wheels moved onto the gravel on the side of the road. Joel quickly pressed the brake peddle with his right foot. The brakes locked up at first, then pulsated as he applied more foot pressure onto the brake peddle. The back wheels were soon riding on the gravel too. Joel's car swayed from side to side, throwing up both dust and stones as it rapidly moved along.

He missed both the car and house trailer, but he couldn't avoid the tree directly in front of him. He managed to slightly reduce the speed of the car, but the impact with the tree was still enough of a problem to break his seat belt and force him to hit his head on the windshield. Joel laid unconscious for more than an hour. The sleeping drunk on the highway never heard any noise, nor did he ever stir from his slumber.

Joel finally regained consciousness. He rubbed his forehead. His fingertips felt wet and sticky. Turning on his interior lights, he looked into the rear view mirror. His vision was blurry. Rubbing both of his eyes with his fingers, he tried blinking them repeatedly. At last his full vision was restored to him. Again he looked into the rear view mirror. There was a knot sized bump on the right side of his forehead. The skin had split and oozed blood. Joel took out his handkerchief from his rear pants pocket and wiped away some of the blood from off his forehead.

Forcing himself out of his car, he had to check the auto's damage. The tree had reshaped the front bumper - - mangled some of the grill work - - and removed one headlight from it's socket. Other than that, the car looked ok.

Joel got back into the car. He turned on the ignition switch. After a few tries, the engine finally started. There was a slight ping - - a loud bang - - then just the sound of a running car engine. It sounded ok to Joel.

Got to find a sheriff's office and make out an accident report for the insurance company, thought Joel. Got to locate one in the next town. He put the gear shift into reverse, looked into the rear view mirror, then backed up onto the highway. He drove off looking for the next town, seeking help for both his head injury and his car.

Rain had begun falling consistently. The windshield wipers rapidly cleared the windows, affording a clear view of the road ahead. Joel drove along for several miles. Eventually, he came upon a small road that turned off of the main highway. A road sign stood erect on the right side of the new road. Joel stopped the car in front of the sign, letting the headlights illuminate it. He silently read to himself:

YOU ARE APPROACHING OBMIL, MONTANA
A GREAT PLACE TO CALL YOUR HOME
POPULATION - - VARIES MONTHLY

That's a crazy sign, thought Joel. But, I mind as well head for that town as any other. Have to find that sheriff's office and a doc for both my head and my car.

Joel drove along the new road. It had finally stopped raining. Bright stars now covered the entire sky. He looked at his wrist watch - - 5:00 a.m.

The sun will be coming up soon, he thought to himself. He passed several farm fields, eventually coming to a crossroad. Joel stopped for the stop sign, then proceeded along slowly. Passing over a set of railroad tracks, he approached some houses.

Must be the start of a town, he thought to himself. Traveling two blocks, he saw an illuminated sign on the front porch of a house on his right. The sign read, *GROGAN'S ROOMING HOUSE - - VACANCY!*

"Aw shit," Joel mumbled aloud, "it's to early to look for a doctor and the sheriff's office. I'll get a room first and rest awhile before I began my search." He stopped the car in front of the rooming house, got out and walked onto the front porch. He knocked on the front door and waited. There was no response. He knocked once - - twice - - and the third time was the charmer. The door opened. An elderly woman of about sixty-five stood in the doorway. The sunlight coming through the windows behind her highlighted the silverness of her hair.

"Can I help you?" she asked, displaying a friendly smile.

"I'm looking for a room to rest in," he replied, looking very exhausted. The woman saw the blood on Joel's forehead.

"*OH,*" she exclaimed, "**YOU'RE *HURT*!**"

"I had a slight auto accident," he replied, touching his forehead with his fingers. "I had a slight disagreement with a large tree. The tree won!"

"Please, come right in," she insisted, stepping aside for him to pass. "Go into the parlor and have a seat. It's on the left as you walk in."

"Thank you," he replied, walking passed her. He entered the parlor. Joel gave the room a quick once over glance. Nothing fancy, he thought, just regular furniture for comfort living. The elderly woman returned, steadily carrying a bowl of warm water, a towel and a small box. She cleansed Joel's wound and applied an antiseptic ointment on it. Joel flinched. The ointment stung at the first application, but then he felt nothing but sootheness. The woman placed a small bandage over the wound. "Should be fine in a few days," she said.

Joel smiled. "Thank you," he replied. "Now," he paused a moment, "I'd like to see the room that you have available."

"I think I can accommodate you," she answered. "You'll like the room. How long do you intend on staying in our little town?" she asked.

"Depends on the circumstances. What's the rent for the room?" he asked.

"Oh," she paused, "we'll decide on that when you decide to leave. Don't worry, the price will be fair. No need to worry about that for now." She paused again. "By the way, my name is Bessie...Bessie Grogan. You can just call me, Bessie. Now mister..." she hesitated. "Just what is your name?" she asked.

"Melenka... Joel Melenka," he replied, "but you can just call me Joel."

"Well Mister Joel Melenka, if you'll just follow me, I'll show you to your room." She stood up and walked towards the staircase that lead to the second floor.

"Just call me, Joel," he remarked as he stood and picked up a small night bag. He followed the elderly woman up the staircase.

CHAPTER II

Joel laid down on top of the soft mattress. In a matter of minutes he was fast asleep. Several hours had passed. The ring from the doorbell woke him up. He looked at his wrist watch. He had been asleep for five hours. Joel felt rested, and he felt refreshed. After washing his face and hands in the bathroom sink, he put on a clean shirt and pants. He left his room and walked down to the first floor. He made a premise check of the entire area.

The dining room table was set for the evening meal. There were eight chairs at the table, but only four place settings were set. Bessie Grogan came out of the kitchen carrying a large bowl of salad.

"*OH!*" she exclaimed, startled by the sight of Joel standing there, watching her. "I trust you had a few hours of rest, Joel?" she asked.

"I feel great," he replied, stretching both arms upwards. "Who are the settings at the table for?" he asked.

"There are two other roomers besides yourself, Joel," she answered, placing the bowl of salad in the middle of the table. "The other setting is for me."

The other two roomers entered the dining room and immediately sat down at the table. They placed their napkins on their laps. They were introduced to Joel as a Mister Wesscot and a Mister Judd. The food was served and eaten quickly without much conversation at the table. The two roomers left the table immediately after they had finished eating.

"That was a fine meal Mrs. Grogan," Joel began. "The roomers didn't say much, but that was some of the best home cooked food that I've tasted in a long time."

"I'm glad you enjoyed it," Bessie Grogan replied, picking up the dirty dishes off of the table.

"Let me help you," Joel offered as he stood up.

"No...no," she protested, "I'll take care of them. It's not a big problem."

"Then, I think I'll take a walk and look over your little town, Bessie," said Joel as he walked to the front door.

"You do that, Mister Melenka. Yes...you do *just* that," she replied, smiling to herself.

CHAPTER III

Joel stepped out onto the front porch. He lit up a cigarette, slowly took a long drag filling his lungs to their capacity, then just as quickly, he let the smoke filter out through his nostrils. He didn't know if Mrs. Grogan aloud smoking in her house. He really didn't want to bother her about it.

Strange, he thought, lately he had a burning sensation in his nostrils when the smoke came through. He even coughed once in awhile after every other drag of the cigarette. But, somehow, today was different. There was no burning sensation and he didn't feel the need to cough after taking a drag on the cigarette. The smoke felt pleasant. His throat didn't burn or feel raspy.

Must be a new brand of tobacco they're using now-a-days, he thought. Got to remember to keep buying this brand of cigarettes. Well, what do I do first? Take a long walk? See about getting the car fixed? Find the sheriff's office and fill out my report for the insurance company? Getting the car fixed won out.

Joel took out his car keys, got into the car and went in search of a repair shop.

He had only traveled a short distance when he came upon a repair garage off of the main street. The shop was located in the middle of the block. Joel pulled into a parking space directly in front of the repair shop and got out of his car. Three men sat in old wooden chairs in front of the doorway leading into the building.

"Good morning," Joel began. "By chance, are one of you gentlemen the owner of this establishment?" he asked.

"I am," said the man on the right. "What can I do for you?" he asked.

"Smashed up the front of my car a little and I want to check it out for other damage too."

"I'd say you smashed it up a lot," said the shop owner. "Well, it's to late to do anything tonight and I took the next two days off. I'll be able to check your car over in about three days. It'll take me a day or so to check it out carefully. I probably could tell you more about the damage in about five days. Of course, if you want me to get you a new bumper and grill, well, that'll be another two weeks or so. I have to send away for all of the parts."

"Don't you have any other help working in your shop?" asked Joel.

"No," replied the shop owner, "I'm the only one that works in my shop."

"And he has the only repair shop in town," said the man in the extreme left chair.

"I'll help you check the car over myself," Joel volunteered.

"No...no sir!" replied the shop owner. "Insurance companies won't permit that. I'm the only one that can be working in my shop."

"What do you propose that I do?" asked Joel.

"Leave the car just where it's at," a pause, "and leave the keys in the ignition too," said the shop owner.

"It'll get stolen out here with the keys in it," shouted Joel.

"Theft in this town is nonexistent," said the shop owner, smiling. "Don't worry about the car."

"OK...OK, I'll do what you say," replied Joel, reluctantly, "but I'm holding you responsible for that car. I've got two witnesses here that heard what you said." All three men smiled without saying another word.

Joel Melenka opened his car door and inserted the key into the ignition switch. He slammed the door and walked away. Every other step, he'd turn around and look back at his car and the three men, muttering words of anger under his breath.

A short walk and he was back on the town's main street. He looked for some kind of a location marker giving the street's name. Finally, he saw a sign on a pole that read - - *CRYSTAL SPRING ROAD*.

"Crystal Spring Road," Joel said aloud, "that's a real nice sounding name for a street." He preceded to walk down the street, passing numerous stores - - hardware, pastry, ice cream, restaurant, bank and novelty shops. One thing he did notice, there were no signs or shops for doctors - - dentists - - clinics - - or hospitals. One other fact caught Joel's attention. All of the stores were closed.

That's strange, thought Joel. It's still light enough to do a little business. Why are they all closed? He did notice that the town had two traffic lights, but the town was lacking the movement of a lot of automobiles. Still have to find that sheriff's office, he reminded himself.

Eventually, he did locate the sheriff's office at the end of the seventh block of his searching endever. Joel tried the doorknob. The door was locked. A large sign pasted on the front plate glass window caught his attention. It read:

> *GONE TO REST.*
> *YOU DO YOUR BEST!*
> *SHERIFF YOTAN.*

"Just what in the hell's going on around here?" Joel said aloud. Well, he thought, tomorrow I'll find the City Hall building and I'll have a talk with one of the officials there. Maybe then, I'll get some of the answers.

Joel put his hands in his front pants pockets and started walking back to the rooming house. He counted twenty-five stores and approximately fifty houses in the small town area.

What a pleasant place this would be to live, he thought as he walked along. You don't hear the crackle of gunfire...No traffic noise...No jackhammers or barking dogs. It's probably a place where children aren't molested or slain on their way to school. Pregnant women, the disabled and the elderly can walk the streets without the worry of being attacked or robbed. That's the impression I've gotten all ready about this town.

Two men and women passed Joel on the sidewalk. They greeted him with a smile and a friendly, *"HELLO."* And yet, several other people passed him by without a smile or uttering a single word after he had said, *"HELLO"* to them. "Strange... it's a strange town," he said to himself again.

He passed the repair shop. His car was still parked out in front of it. The three men were still sitting in their chairs, smiling. Joel just shook his head and smiled to himself.

Eventually he reached the rooming house and went directly to his room and went to bed. He was totally exhausted from the long days' activities.

CHAPTER IV

Bessie Grogan's breakfast call woke Joel Melenka up at 7:00 a.m. He showered and shaved, then dressed for breakfast.

Entering the dining room, he saw two new faces - - a man and a woman. Bessie Grogan came into the dining room carrying a large platter of pork sausages and hot pancakes.

"How did you know I loved sausages and hot pancakes for breakfast?" asked Joel after he sat down at the table. He placed his napkin on his lap.

"Oh," began Bessie Grogan, pausing a moment, "I know more about you than you think," she said as she sat down at the table.

"Where are the two gentlemen that I met yesterday?" Joel asked.

"They had to leave early this morning to catch the early morning bus out of Obmil," answered Bessie Grogan. She introduced the two people sitting at the table to Joel. "This is Mrs. Alene Gusick and Mister Carl Hatch. They arrived on the early bus this morning. They'll be staying with us for a short while."

"Glad to meet you both," said Joel, standing up and shaking both person's hands. They responded the same way. The conversation at the table was again minimal. For some reason, Joel felt both uneasy and uncomfortable. He asked very reasonable questions and was given very vague answers.

Joel quickly finished his breakfast, bid the new roomers farewell and left the rooming house. Standing on the front porch, he looked at his wrist watch - - 9:00 a.m. He glanced up at the sky. It was a cool water blue in color without a cloud anywhere in sight. The slight breeze that touched his face felt warm and inviting. The sun's bright rays enhanced the beauty of the green grass and colorful flowers that decorated the front of the rooming house. Birds began to both chirp and sing a melodious tune as they perched on the branches in the tree tops.

It's gonna be another great day, thought Joel. He placed his hands in his front pants pockets, walked down the stairs, then headed towards the main part of town in search of City Hall.

He soon reached the section of town that had the first traffic light. He looked down the street on his right. His car was still in the street in front of the repair shop. The three men sat in their chairs on the sidewalk. Joel decided to walk over to them and engage in some friendly conversation.

"Good mornin, gents" he began, "fine lookin day, isn't it?" he asked.

"It certainly is," said the middle man.

"Say gents," Joel continued, "I'm looking for City Hall or your Records Administration Building. Can you help me out?"

"Just turn around," said the man on the right, "and keep walking for two blocks. You can't miss it. It's a big white brick building on the right side of the street."

Joel thanked them and bid them a good day and started his search for the big white brick building. After walking the suggested two blocks, there it was, right where the gentleman said it would be. Joel walked up three concrete steps and entered the building through the glass doorway. People moved about, but said nothing. There were no sounds of ringing phones.

That's strange for a public building, thought Joel. This quiet is astounding. He saw a young woman seated at a large, light oak colored desk at the far end of the room. He approached the woman.

"Good morning, miss," he began, "my name is..."

"Mister Joel Melenka," she replied, interrupting him.

Joel was momentarily stunned. He didn't know this woman from Adam. How did she know who he was? When the temporary shock wore off, Joel continued speaking. "How do you know who I am?" he asked.

"This is a small town, Mister Melenka," she replied. "Not much goes on around here that everyone doesn't know about. People come and go, but we get to meet all of them eventually." She smiled. "And I suppose you want to see Mayor Niam Legna this morning?"

"Mayor Legna?" Joel hesitated, then said, "why yes, I'd like to see Mayor Legna."

"He's been expecting you," said the woman. "Go right into his office."

What in the hell? thought Joel. This is sure one hell-of-a-friendly town. He smiled at the woman, said, "thank you," and walked into Mayor Legna's office.

A husky man, with snow white hair, a clear complexion and a friendly smile, sat behind a large desk. Before him, on top of the desk, was a large register book. It looked quite old by the looks of the binding. It appeared that the mayor was reading a page in the book. When he saw Joel approaching, he closed the book and stood up. He outstretched his right hand towards Joel. Joel grasped it with his right hand.

"Good morning Mayor Legna," he said.

After shaking hands, the mayor sat down. "Please sit down Mister Melenka," said the mayor. Joel obliged him. He let the mayor speak first before he started spouting out questions that he wanted answers too.

The mayor continued. "I'm glad you came in to see me this morning."

"Yea, well," Joel interrupted, "I was looking for the sheriff to make out an accident report for my insurance company. You see, the other night I had..."

"An accident," interrupted the mayor. "Yes I know, but unfortunately our sheriff has left town and we have no one to fill the vacancy at the moment.

Say, how about you, Mister Melenka? You've been in law enforcement. How about taking over the sheriffs job and living in our little town with us?"

Joel was again stunned by the offer. This was a nice peaceful town, but it was also a strange town. This is nuts, thought Joel before he spoke. "What in the hell is going on?" he asked directly. "Look Mayor Legna, I just want to fill out an accident report and be on my merry way after my car gets fixed."

"Well," said the mayor, "there you are! Take the job until your car gets fixed and then you can go on from there. At least our town will have a peace officer to protect it."

Holy shit, what in the hell am I getting myself into, thought Joel as he wiped his forehead with his handkerchief. Before he realized what he was doing, he had said, "*YES*," to the mayor's request and accepted the position of sheriff. Mayor Legna came out from behind his desk and pinned a badge on Joel's shirt.

"Don't you have to swear me in with some kind of a ceremony?" asked Joel.

"Oh, we'll just forget the formalities," answered the mayor. "We're all friends in this town and we trust each other."

"Then why do you need a sheriff?" asked Joel.

"For the heavy bus traffic," answered the mayor.

"The heavy bus traffic?" said Joel, having a puzzled expression on his face.

"Oh, just never mind that for now" interrupted the mayor, "you'll see for yourself soon enough. Now, here are the keys for the sheriff's office and the town's one police car. And, with that Sheriff Melenka, I will have to bid you a good-day sir as I have a busy schedule to attend this morning."

Joel accepted the keys, shook hands with the mayor and left the white brick building before he realized what was happening. He stood out on the sidewalk, dumbfounded, staring at the keys' lying in the palm of his hand.

"*What in the hell did I just do?*" he said aloud. He thought, I must be nuts to have accepted this job. I don't want to work anymore. I just want to fish... read...watch TV...and just take it easy. What have I gotten myself into? He shrugged his shoulders and decided to look for an answer in the sheriff's office.

CHAPTER V

Joel cleaned up the office and the town's one police car. Next, he rummaged through the papers in the desk and file cabinets. He found nothing of interest to him.

The following four weeks that followed had crazy filled events for Joel. He just shunned them off as natural events for this strange town. His car was still parked out in front of the repair shop. The parts for it still hadn't come to town.

The boundaries for the sheriff's jurisdiction for the town was another strange informative piece of information - - one mile north of the town to War Eagle Road - - one mile south of the town to Moose Lake Road - - two miles east of the town to Tower Road - - and two miles west of the town to Panthersville Road.

It would only take Joel an hour or two to patrol the entire sector of his jurisdiction. The rest of the time he would spend visiting with the shop owners, that was when the shops were briefly open. Not many customers came into the stores. Joel wondered how these shop owners were able to survive without many purchases being made.

Automobile activity in the town was minimal, but the bus traffic was extremely heavy. New people arrived daily on the morning and noon time bus arrivals. And, just as many people left on the night time bus schedules. With all the coming and going, the amount of people always seemed to balance out. The town was never extremely overcrowded, only desolate in the early morning hours when Joel patrolled the streets.

The roomers, in his rooming house, never stayed longer than two days. But, the shop keepers were always the same people, while the people occupying the small houses surrounding the town, came and went, bi-weekly.

One afternoon, in the middle of the fifth week, Joel Melenka sat with the three men in front of the auto repair shop. He was trying to convince the shop owner to hurry the repairs on his car because he wanted to leave this town.

During their conversation, a large bus stopped at the corner of Crystal Spring Road. Joel watched as two adults and fifthy children walked off of the bus. The children were laughing and running around the bus, playing tag. Mayor Legna approached the bus driver. They spoke momentarily, then the mayor removed a small notebook and pen from his coat pocket. He compared the list, that the bus driver had given to him, with the notes in his notebook. He finished, smiled and put the notebook and pen back into his coat pocket. The children ran around the mayor, forming a circle. The mayor patted one of the children on the head and told her to be careful, but to have fun playing. Joel stood up and walked over to the bus.

"Afternoon, Mayor," he said smiling.

"Afternoon Sheriff Melenka," answered the mayor. "Finished with all of your official duties this morning?" he asked.

"Just taking it easy for awhile. What's with all the children Mayor? Where are they headed? Don't see any parents with them?"

"Oh," replied Mayor Legna, "we've a special camp for children a few miles west of town near Panthersville Road."

"I've patrolled that area several times," said Joel, "but I don't remember running across any kind of a camp around there?"

"Sure there is," insisted the mayor, "you just didn't look around hard enough. Lots of trees and shrubbery around there you know. You just missed it...that's all!"

The children boarded the bus. Within minutes, the bus was on its' way.

Joel waited several hours after the bus and the children left town. He wanted to finish patrolling the area before the sun set. Traveling up and down Panthersville Road, he searched both sides of the road and still was unable to locate that children's camp.

Mayor must have given me the wrong directions, thought Joel. Oh well, no harm done.

Joel never paid any attention to the names on the front of the buses that entered and left the town. He really didn't care were they were coming from or what their final destination would be.

CHAPTER VI

The beginning of the sixth week, Joel and a shop owner sat on chairs out on the sidewalk in front of the store. Joel leaned back on his chair, balancing himself on the back two legs. They were discussing Joel's car problems. The car was still parked in front of the auto repair shop, and the parts still hadn't come in.

A large bus slowly approached, stopping next to the curb, directly in front of them. Joel read the destination sign on the bus register - - *OBMIL, MONTANA*. He watched as several people got off of the bus, and just as many boarded the bus to leave town.

Wonder where they're all going? Thought Joel. The bus driver closed the bus door and changed the destination sign on the front of the bus. It read - - *HEYVANSBOUND, MONTANA*.

Never heard of that town, though Joel. I've got to look it up on a map and see where that town is in relation to this town. It may be a nice spot to visit, or maybe even live. The bus was on its' way out of town in a matter of minutes.

An hour had passed. Several people had started to gather at the corner bus stop. Another bus was soon to pull up in front of Joel and the shop owner.

This time, no one had gotten off of the bus. At least, by Joel's quick count, twenty people had boarded the bus.

Strange, thought Joel. None of these people are carrying suitcases or small carry on luggage. The destination sign on the bus read - - *OBMIL, MONTANA* when it arrived. After the people had boarded the bus, the driver changed the destination sign, just as the other bus driver had done. It read - - *SEYTONSWELL, MONTANA*. Another strange town's name, thought Joel. I'll have to look on the map for that town too.

CHAPTER VII

It was on Tuesday morning of the seventh week that Joel had encountered still another strange experience. By the hands on his wrist watch, it was 10:00 a.m. None of the shops were open on Crystal Spring road. Joel had tried all of the shop's doors. They were all locked. No one stirred in any of the stores.

Dressed in his sheriff's uniform, Joel gave careful eye surveillance to the entire area. He sat down on the sidewalk bench near the bus stop. A half hour passed. A bus approached the designated parking area for buses.

Joel stood up and approached the bus. He read the destination sign - - *OBMIL, MONTANA*.. Several people got off of the bus. No one was at the bus stop to get on the bus. The driver shut the door and quickly changed the destination sign to read - - *SEYTONSWELL, MONTANA*. He started the bus and quickly drove away.

Joel decided to welcome everyone to Obmil. After all, he was one of the town's officials. As he approached the group of people, he was stopped in his tracks. He recognized one of the men standing in the crowd. Joel approached the man with an outstretched hand, offering a friendly handshake.

"DICK! DICK CRANE!" Joel shouted. The man looked blankly at Joel.

"Do you know me?" asked the man. "Do you know who I am?"

"Of course I know who you are," replied Joel. "Why hell man, you and I grew up together. Sure, we haven't seen each other in the last few years, but hell, why in the hell wouldn't I remember one of my best friends?"

"I don't remember my name," the man replied again, "or who I am...or where I came from. I don't know what happened to me or just why I'm here in this town holding this bus ticket."

Joel led the man over to the wooden bench. They both sat down. Joel began the conversation. "Look, your name is Richard Crane. You were born in Chicago and we grew up together. We attended the same schools and we were inseparable friends. Then, we both got married and went our separate ways. Think hard Dick! Try to remember anything that happened to you."

Dick Crane's forehead wrinkled as he tried to force his brain to bring forth some kind of information for him to remember. After several minutes, Dick Crane said, "I remember being in a hospital getting some medical tests for a medical problem that I had. I remember having to go to the bathroom. My bladder felt as though it were going to burst. I forced myself off of the bed and started walking towards the bathroom. The next thing that I remember is standing in line with a bunch of people, waiting for a bus to pick us up. I was dressed in these jeans, plaid sport shirt and sandals. After waiting a short while, a bus pulls up in front of us and stops. The driver opened the front door and a man got off of the bus. He began helping people to board the bus. When it came to my turn, he smiled and handed me this ticket. He said it was my transportation ticket to Obmil, Montana and also onto my next stop which was to be my final destination.

"Can I see the ticket, Dick?" asked Joel.

"Sure...here," said Dick Crane, handing the piece of paper to Joel.

Joel examined the piece of paper. It was blank, with only a single punch hole in the center of it. He turned the paper over to the other side. That side was blank too.

"I don't see this paper being of any value to you, Dick," said Joel, handing the piece of paper back to his friend. Dick Crane held the piece of paper tightly in his right hand. They chatted several minutes. Nothing really got accomplished in solving Dick Crane's problems. They continued talking. It was during this time that Joel noticed more people starting to gather at the bus stop.

After a passing hour, another bus approached the bus stop. The driver opened the buses front door. "*ALL ABOARD!*" he shouted as he changed the destination sign from - - *OBMIL* to *HEYVANSVILL, MONTANA.*

The people began boarding the bus. Dick Crane stood up and started walking towards the buses front door without saying another word to Joel.

"Where are you going?" asked Joel, grabbing hold of his friend's arm. "Stay here with me Dick. I'm staying at a nice rooming house and they always have plenty of room there. You don't have to worry about the rent. You can square up with Bessie Grogan when you decide to leave. If you're broke, I'll stake you until you can get your memory back."

Dick Crane pulled his arm away from his friend's grasp. *"I've got to board this bus,"* he shouted. *"I don't know why, or where it's going, but I just know that I have to be on this bus!"*

Dick Crane boarded the bus without saying another word - - not even good-bye to his friend. The bus driver shut the door and drove off leaving Joel Melenka standing alone at the bus stop.

"*THAT'S IT!*" Joel shouted angrily, "*I've had it! I'm gonna get down to the bottom of what's going on in this crazy town!*"

Joel walked away from the bus stop, storming towards City Hall. Upon entering the large white brick building, he walked directly over to the mayor's secretary.

"Listen," he began, "I want to see the ...." Before he could finish his sentence, the secretary said, "go right in Sheriff Melenka. The Mayor is expecting you."

Joel was dumbfounded. That was another thing. Everyone knew what he was going to do before he knew what he was going to do. "Here we go again," he mumbled to himself. He stormed into the Mayor's office. Pointing his index finger directly at the mayor, who was sitting behind his desk, smiling, he said, "listen Mayor, I want to get to....." Before he could finish the sentence, the mayor interrupted him.

"Sit down, Joel," the mayor began. "We'll have our talk right now. It's about time that we did. I surely thought that by this time you would have figured out everything by yourself."

"*Figure out what?*" exclaimed Joel.

"This town...the people...the bus transportation,"the mayor continued. "And, haven't you lost your appetite for food in the last few weeks?" he asked.

"Yea, but I just thought it was my way of cutting down on my eating habits. You know, when you get older you're suppose to have a less of a yearn for the taste of food."

"We all went through that phase when we were here for awhile, Joel. Soon you won't want any food at all."

"Will you kindly explain to me Mayor, just what in the hell is going on?" Joel asked again.

The mayor sat back in his easy chair, pyramiding his fingers together. He smiled. "Joel," he began, "this town exists only for the people who can relate to it. The town is like a sanctuary. Sort of a haven for," he paused, "for people's souls. In the world of the living, only the roads and crossroads exist here. To the living, there is no town existing here."

"*WHAT!*" exclaimed Joel. "*ARE YOU NUTS?*"

"Joel, just listen carefully to what I have to say to you," requested the mayor. "Just hear me out."

Joel felt himself calming down. "Go ahead, Mayor. I'm listening," he replied.

"First of all, your car is just an illusion. It will never be repaired. It will always remain in front of the auto repair shop for appearance sake. Our town's name is self-explanatory. If you reverse the letters in the name, you will come up with the town's real name - - *LIMBO!* That's exactly what this town is, a way station between heaven and hell. Both places are momentarily filled to capacity. Expansion settlements have to be arranged for the new souls that are going to both places. The damned will eventually go to hell. The souls that go to heaven...well...some stay there and other souls are placed into the bodies of new born babies.

"Just as your body has lost the taste for food, your needs for material things will lessen with each day that you are here with us. It's not so bad living here. Why, I've been here," the mayor paused, "oh let's just say for a long time. The rooming house and shop keepers are permanent residents here. That's their destiny. They chose to stay here and help others on their way. My name, if you reverse the letters spells out the name...."

"*MAIN ANGEL*," Joel interrupted. "I was thinking about that while you were talking. What about those children and the day camp?" he asked.

"They're all at their final destination now...heaven," said the mayor.

"So," Joel paused, "you're saying that I'm dead?"

"That's right son. But, with you, we have a slight problem."

"*SHIT*!" Joel shouted, then hesitated. "I'm sorry. I mean *HECK*. Never mind the problem, just tell me when I can leave and what bus do I take?"

"The buses go to two places," continued the mayor. "The bus that goes directly to heaven is labeled....*HEYVANSBOUND*. The bus that goes directly to hell is labeled....*SEYTONSWELL*. But," the mayor paused, "you're not going to be boarding neither of those buses."

"*What*!" exclaimed Joel. "*Why?*" he asked concerningly.

"You died in that auto accident, Joel. The car caught fire and then exploded. But, it wasn't your time to die. You couldn't be sent back because your human body was disintergrated. You have to stay here with us. It was decided, by the *MAN* upstairs, that you be given the sheriff's job and stay with us until the date that you were due to die. You were suppose to go to a place that was closer to hell and wait there. But because, just like you, an elderly woman stopped by the spot where you died to say a short prayer for your soul, you came here to us. That single prayer was just enough to get you up here to *Limbo*."

"Then I'm stuck here until a date that I'll never know?" asked Joel.

"Yes," answered the mayor, "only I and the *MAN* upstairs knows when that date is. You see Joel, it always does help to say a *short prayer for a stranger!*"

THE SIZZLING SOUND

CHAPTER I

Several speed boats skimmed across the water in the center of Chalters Lake, pulling water skiers closely behind them. At the extreme north end of the lake a dredging machine slowly probes the lakes muddy bottom. Several people are standing on a pier, watching the machinery in operation. The local sheriff's car, with its' mars lights flashing the emergency signal, stopped next to the pier with a screeching halt.

"Mornin," Sheriff Haines," said one of the watchers.

"Morning, Sy," replied the sheriff.

"Another one's missin, Sheriff," continued Sy. "That makes the tenth one this month. We found the boat overturned near the edge of the Lilly pads."

"Yep, I know," answered Sheriff Haines "We got the call this morning. Who's the missing person?" he asked.

"Better ask Vodka-John, Sheriff," said Sy. He kin tell you more than me."

Vodka-John appeared in the lodge's front doorway, then walked towards the pier. "Morning, Sheriff," he said as he tried to button his checkered colored sport shirt that was much too small to cover his large midriff bulge. "Came out when I saw your squad car pull up."

"Morning, Vodka-John. How about giving me some information on the missing man?"

Vodka-John ran his stubby fingers through his sandy colored hair, pulling the long strands away from his half awakened eyes. "He was a city feller... tall... nice lookin... Oh yes, he's a nice dresser too. Came here to do a little fishin."

"Did he have any friends or relatives with him when he arrived here?" asked the sheriff.

Taking a cigarette out of his cigarette pack from his shirt pocket, Vodka-John lit it and took a long slow drag. As he exhaled, the wind quickly whisked the smoke away from his face, blowing it in different directions.

"Said he was alone when he checked in," Vodka-John continued. "Didn't see anyone else with him. Said he was a writer from Chicago working on a new book. He liked the looks of this place and decided to settle here for a spell. Liked to do a little fishin too, so he said."

Sheriff Haines wrote down the information in his little black notebook that he removed from his back pants pocket. Together, the two men walked to the end of the pier. Sheriff Haines perched his butt on top of one of the short dock posts and continued his questioning. "Already talked with Sy,

Vodka-John, but he couldn't give me much information. Mind answering a few more questions?"

Vodka-John leaned against a dock post and puffed on his cigarette. "Sure Sheriff, ask away," he replied.

"What's the missing man's name?"

"Sam... Sam Kenders...That's what he signed in the register book."

"When did he arrive?"

"Let's see, about a week ago, on Tuesday."

"Can you give me a brief description of what he looks like? I'd like to see if he's wanted or missing from another state."

"Well," continued Vodka-John, rubbing his chubby chin as he watched the white clouds pass overhead, "he's about six foot tall, with dark curly hair, blue eyes and built very thin. Didn't look like he enjoyed food very much. Nothing else unusual about him that I can remember. That's about all that I can tell you about him, sheriff."

"That'll be enough for a start. Oh, one more thing, Vodka-John. Did you by chance hear or see anything unusual last night?"

"Well, let's see," Vodka-John rubbed his chin, then raised one eyebrow. "It was about 7:00 p.m. last night. I was tending bar. The place was empty except for three people sitting at the bar. Mr. Kenders came in and asked if he could borrow a boat, motor and some fishing bait. Said he was working on a new chapter for his book. He thought that being alone on the lake would help him to gather his thoughts. I gave him what he asked for, he thanked me, left the bar, got into the speed boat, started the engine and headed out towards the center of the lake. We all heard the engine running for awhile, then it stopped. For a long time there was nothing but silence.

"Then we all heard this horrible scream followed by a loud splash. You know how sound travels across a quiet lake at night. Well, I ran out of the bar, followed by the three customers. We all ran out to the end of the pier. It was really to dark to see anything. The only thing that we did hear was a very loud sizzling sound. It was like someone had put a hot poker into a bucket of cold water. Know what I mean, sheriff!" he asked.

"Yes, I know," answered Sheriff Haines.

The sheriff finished writing down his notes in his notebook. He looked up at Vodka-John and asked, "Are you finished?"

"Yep...I'm afraid that's it, Sheriff," he said.

"Well, I guess that's about all I can do around here. I'll do some investigating around the lake area. Maybe I'll get lucky and come up with something else. Could be someone saw something unusual last night. Well, Vodka-John, thanks for all of your help. Talk to you later." Sheriff Haines slid his butt off of the dock post that he was sitting on and walked towards his car.

"*O.K. SHERIFF. GLAD TO HELP YOU ANYTIME,*" yelled Vodka-John. He waved good-bye with one hand and tried to button his shirt with the other hand.

II

The sheriff entered his squad car, turned on the ignition and sped down the dirt road, leaving a cloud of swirling dust behind him. Driving along, he thought, what in the hell is happening around here? This is the tenth person to disappear this month. Haven't had this much trouble around here since that incident four years ago when a couple of kids stole old man Silke's cow. Darn near drove the old man nuts looking everywhere for that damn cow. I've got to come up with an answer, and I have to do it pretty soon. Election is coming up again next month. I'd better solve this mystery if I ever expect to be elected sheriff again.

Sheriff Haines circled the lake area the rest of the afternoon, stopping at different homes, questioning everyone that he came in contact with. No one had really seen anything unusual. The only thing that was mentioned by several people was hearing a strange sizzling sound that had started over a month ago. The strange noise always occurred late in the evening. Several people even stated that they had heard it on ten different occasions.

Sheriff Haines was still puzzled. He drove to the section of the lake where the Lilly pads covered the top of the water like a green carpet with little white flowered designs sprinkled around in an irregular pattern. He stopped the squad car, got out, lit up a cigarette and sat down on a dry rotted log. The parts of the puzzle formed a circular pattern going through his mind. How do ten people just disappear? Their boats had been found over turned in this particular section of the lake. No traces of their bodies were ever found. And what was that strange sizzling sound that everyone had heard? What significant part of the investigation did the sound play in the mystery of the missing people? How does everything fit together?

Sheriff Haines shook his head. He was disgusted. His eyes slowly scanned the entire lake area. He felt heat on his finger tips as his cigarette neared its end. Flipping the cigarette into the lake, he got up off of the log and went back to his squad car. Pausing for a moment, his eyes again scanned the entire lake.

There's only one thing that I can do, he thought to himself, and that's the fact that I have to close up the lake area. Stop everyone from using the lake until I solve this damn mystery. The sheriff entered the squad car, started the engine and drove off in the direction of town.

III

The next morning, bright and early, Sheriff Haines went to the town's only print shop. He ordered two hundred *NO TRESPASSING* signs to be printed up as soon as possible. The sheriff's entire afternoon was spent tacking signs on the trees around the entire lake area.

It was 9:35 p.m. when the sheriff's car finally approached Vodka-John's resort lodge. He went into the bar portion of the lodge. Some people were seated at the bar, while a few sat at the tables in the back of the room. The jukebox blared loud music, drowning out the voices of the people.

"Hi, Sheriff," said Vodka-John, smiling, as he wiped the top of the bar off with a damp terry cloth towel. "Have any luck solving the mystery yet?" he asked.

Sheriff Haines walked over to the bar and sat down on a leather covered bar stool. He took off his hat and placed it on the empty bar stool next to him.

"Nothing yet," he replied. "I'd like to borrow some of your equipment for tonight, Vodka-John. Think I'm gonna go out on the lake tonight for awhile."

"Goin out there by yourself, Sheriff?" asked one of the patrons sitting at the opposite end of the bar.

"Yep. I've got to unravel this mystery somehow. Maybe by me being out on the lake tonight, might help to find some kind of an answer."

"What'll you need, Sheriff?" asked Vodka-John.

"Your fastest speed boat with the large beacon light on it. I'll need an extra long length of rope too. I'll give you a voucher for the items that I take so you'll be compensated for them if anything gets damaged or lost. I'll be taking along my service revolver and a thirty-thirty rifle. That should stop anything that I might run across.

Vodka-John turned around and removed a set of keys off of a hook screwed into the wall. He threw them on the bar in front of the sheriff.

"Here you are, Sheriff. She's all yours. Lots of luck on your venture. Hope you find what your looking for."

Sheriff Haines picked up the keys and left the bar. He boarded the speed boat, started the motor, untied the rope fastened around the dock post and headed for the center of Chaulters Lake. He traveled the same route that the missing persons supposedly had taken.

Sheriff Haines turned of the engine and drifted around the center of the lake for what seemed like an eternity. Nothing happened. He again started the engine and began going around in large circles. Still nothing unusual occurred. Two and a half hours had passed. The sheriff became discouraged.

Maybe I'll go over to the Lilly pads where the other boats were found, he thought. He gave the steering wheel a half turn and headed the boat for the Lilly pad infested area of the lake.

Traveling along the water for a few minutes, he finally arrived at the edge of the Lilly pads. Shutting of the boat's engine, he sat and waited for something to happen. Nothing. He sat back and looked up at the cloudless sky.

There was a bright half moon glowing up in the sky. The bright stars twinkled against the skies dark background, resembling a twinkling diamond necklace. The lake was calm.

Suddenly, the boat began to be drawn towards the center of the Lilly pad field.

Better get out of here, thought Sheriff Haines. Once you get stuck in these pads, it takes an act of God to get you out of here. He started the engine and threw the clutch control into reverse. The boat began to move back slowly. It only traveled a few feet when the engine strained itself and then quite running. It was as if something was holding the propeller back from turning.

Sheriff Haines pressed the starter button over and over. The engine wouldn't start. Then came the sizzling sound. It started as a soft whisper, gradually getting louder and louder. The water surrounding the boat became illuminated. The plants that the sheriff had thought were Lilly pads had developed a phosphorus glow. A scratching noise came from the bottom of the boat. It started in one spot - - then another - - and still another.

The sheriff turned on the spotlight and pointed it at the bow of the boat. For some crazy unknown reason, the green pads had seemed to be coming alive. They started to engulf the boat from all directions. The white flowers grew in both size and height. The petals got larger while the stems grew higher - - one inch - - two inches - - a foot - - two feet!

Sheriff Haines frantically pressed the engine's starter button. The engine wouldn't catch. A cluster of green pads wrapped themselves around his right ankle. He tried to pull them off, but the attempt was futile. The sizzling sound grew louder and louder. A loud schrill scream came from behind him. He quickly spun around. There before him was a large Lilly pad, the size of a large watermelon. It grabbed his left arm and held on to it.

The sheriff tried to pull himself free. His attempts were useless. He felt the flesh slowly being peeled from his arm.

"*MY GOD,*" he screamed, "*THESE PLANTS ARE CANNIBALISTIC PLANTS... NOT WATER LILIES.*"

Sheriff Haines drew his revolver from his holster and managed to fire off two shots. The small metal projectiles passed through the plants like they were made of paper. Bullets were useless in trying to stop them.

The sizzling sounds got louder and louder. Another giant white flower sprang up from under the water and grabbed the sheriff's right arm. His revolver fell into the water. He felt his very existence slowly being extracted from his body.

"*ON MY GOD, SOMEBODY PLEASE HELP ME. HELP ME GET AWAY,* "*he* screamed, "*I'VE GOT TO TELL EVERYONE ABOUT THEM.*"

The sheriff's screams for help were cut short with the help of a giant water flower that engulfed the upper half portion of his body, pulling Sheriff Haines into the water and capsizing the speed boat.

The following day the dredging machines were back at work, dragging the bottom of the lake for Sheriff Haines body. Two men stood on the pier belonging to Vodka-John's resort.

"Yes officer," said Vodka-John, "Sheriff Haines is the eleventh person to disappear this month."

"Did you notice anything unusual about last night?" asked the State Trooper.

"No.....," Vodka-John hesitated a moment and rubbed his chin with his right hand, "the only thing I heard last night, officer, was just a loud sizzling sound!"

SECRETS OF SILENT LAKE
CHAPTER I

The single engine Piper Cub airplane slowly scanned the tall tree tops. Its pontoons glistened in the bright sunlight. The roar of the engine echoed off of the still water from the silent lake below. The planes two passengers searched vigorously for any signs of life. There was none visible. Not one single animal could be seen. The small plane circled the lake several times.

"Well, there it is, Jim. That's the lake I spotted while on patrol yesterday when I flew off course."

"You were right, Bob. This lake isn't charted on any of our maps. I'll call back to camp and confirm this find." Jim flicked on the radio switch located at the top of the plane's dashboard.

"This is Q-R-763 calling H-Q-492, base camp." Jim repeated the call signals. "This is Q-R-763 calling H-Q-492, base camp. Come in please. Over."

The radio's speakers replied back with only static. Jim repeated his call signal again. Still no reply came back.

"We're to far off course to reach anyone on this radio. Circle the area once more and then head back for our base camp. We'll make our report then. Take the plane down a little lower this time. Maybe we'll see something at a lower altitude?"

"Did you log the altitude and longitude coordinates of the lake, Jim?" asked Bob Goodlow.

"Yes, 120 degrees Southwest by 46 degrees Northeast," answered Jim Graves. "Try the radio once more, Jim." Jim Graves repeated the call for the third time as the plane descended to a lower altitude.

Bob readjusted the gasoline mixture, but not quick enough. The top of one of the taller trees punctured the plane's fuselage and elevator controls, snapping two of the guide wires.

"*JIM, USE THE RADIO AGAIN,*" Bob shouted as he tried to level out the planes glide pattern. "*USE THE EMERGENCY FREQUENCY. SEE IF YOU CAN REACH ANYONE? KEEP GIVING OUT OUR LOCATION.*" Jim followed Bob's instructions.

"Mayday...Mayday! This is Q-R-763. Mayday...Mayday! Plane being forced down at 120 degrees Southwest by 46 degrees Northeast. Mayday.... Mayday!"

Jim Graves repeated the distress call over and over again. The airplane developed a strong vibration.

"Can't gain any altitude, Jim. We'll have to find a place to set her down. I don't have any elevator controls." The airplane was still descending rapidly. Bob continued speaking. "We're right in the path of the lake. We've only got a minute or so. I think I'll be able to set her down. Cross your fingers buddy and maybe kiss your ass good-bye ... cause here we *GO-O-O!*"

The nose of the airplane dipped. Bob Goodlow struggled with the control wheel, trying to keep the airplane as level and on course as he possibly could. The plane swayed from right to left, descending rapidly.

The airplane's pontoons finally made contact with the water. The plane skimmed across the top of the water, kicking up a large mist spray behind it. Bob reversed the engine, forcing it to act as a brake to reduce their speed. The airplane finally slowed down. It rocked back and forth with the waters motion

"You did it, Bob. God-damn, we made it," Jim shouted happily.

Bob Graves said nothing. His hands shook as he held onto the control wheel. He ran his fingers through his thick black curly hair and smiled at his partner. Several drops of perspiration fell from his forehead. His legs felt like rubber. This was the first time that Bob Graves had to make a landing under these kind of conditions.

Both men remained motionless in their seats, taking a few moments to steady their nerves. The plane had successfully landed in the center of this silent lake.

"Try the radio again, Jim. Maybe that rough landing shook it up a bit. Could be that someone will hear us now." Jim spoke the same distress calls. He tried repeatedly. No reply came back. Only static.

"We'd better cool it for now with the radio, Jim. We've got to save those batteries. We'll try again tonight. The first thing we've got to do is get this damn plane to the shore line."

"There's a small clearing over there to your left," said Jim, pointing towards the shore. "See it?" he asked. Bob looked over his left shoulder.

"Yea, I see it," he replied.

"Have you any rope, Bob? I could attach one end to the eyelet on the pontoons and tie the other end around my waist. I'll try to pull the plane while I swim towards shore."

"You'd be too exhausted, Jim. You'd only make it half way before you had to give it up. The distance is to far."

"Well, I'm open to suggestions, Bob?"

"If I run the engine at a low speed, I should be able to guide the plane over to that clearing. I can use the rudder for steering."

"You'll have to use up a lot of the batteries juice to start up that engine again. It'll take a lot out of it."

"Jim, we've got to take that chance. Right now, it's the only one we've got."

II

Bob turned on the ignition switch, twisted the gas valve and pressed the starter button. The engine labored as the propeller turned slowly. Nothing happened. The engine wouldn't start. Bob turned all the switches off and waited a few minutes. He turned the switches back on and pressed the starter button. Again the engine labored as the propeller turned. At last, the engine started. Bob pulled the control back slowly, giving the engine more gas as the propeller spun around faster. The airplane began to slowly move forward. Bob held the control wheel and worked the rudder controls with his feet, right to left, left to right, again and again

They finally reached the clearing. Bob Graves turned off the engine. Jim forced the door open on his side of the plane. He stood on the pontoon, then jumped onto the shore. Using a rope that he found in a small locker under his seat, he tied one end to the metal eyelet that was attached to the pontoon. Bob opened his door, stood on the other pontoon and proceeded to give Jim a hand in securing the plane to the shore line. They fastened the rope around two large oak trees.

"There, that should hold it," said Bob, "let's see how bad our damage is?"

They examined the plane from the nose to the rear tail. The tree had torn a one foot, six inch hole in the bottom of the fuselage. It also made a jagged rip in the elevator and split the control cables.

"*WOW-EEEEEE!*" said Jim, whistling. "Will you look at that! How in the hell will we be able to repair that?" he asked.

"I don't know," replied Bob, shaking his head from side to side, "but, we'll have to try something if we ever want to get out of this place."

"We mind as well set up camp right here. I'll get some equipment from the plane, Jim. You start gathering some wood. We'll need a big fire tonight. Can't tell what kind of animals live around here."

Fifteen minutes later, Jim was back at the clearing with an arm load of branches and broken tree limbs. Bob was seated on a large smooth gray rock. Jim dropped the wood on the ground.

"This should be enough to get us through the night. If you don't think so, I'll gather more later. Find anything useful in the plane?"

"Not too much. A first aid kit, a few tools, a flare gun and two flares, some more rope, an ax and our revolvers."

"Find any extra ammo?"

"No, just what we have in the guns. That's it."

"What about food?"

"I brought along two sandwiches in case I got hungry while on patrol. That's the only food we've got."

"We'd better start thinking about getting more food. I've got a funny feeling that we're gonna be here for a little while."

III

The rest of the day was spent in preparing for nightfall. A shelter was made from the gathering of small trees and branches. More wood was cut for the fire.

Night time had finally arrived. The light from the flickering fire helped Bob see the time on his wrist watch... 10:30 p.m.

"Should we give the radio another try, Jim?" asked Bob.

"We haven't tried it since this afternoon. Mind as well give it one try. Don't use the batteries for more than a minute. We'll have to conserve them."

Bob switched on the radio transmitter. He broadcast their distress signal for only one moment. They received no reply, only static. Bob turned the radio off. They both agreed to bunk down for the night.

The silence of the night was suddenly disturbed by strange noises that surrounded them. Strange sounds that they had never heard before.

"Should we investigate?" asked Bob.

"Better wait till morning. We'll be able to see better then," replied Jim as his hand tightened on the grip of his revolver.

The vision of a million stars illuminated the sky. They laid on their grass beds, both looking up at the sky. The sky resembled a diamond necklace gleaming with a twinkling brilliance. The smoke from their camp fire rose upward, forming large ringlets.

It's been quite a day, thought Bob. He closed his eyes and fell fast asleep.

IV

Night passed. The early morning rays of daylight broke through the tall tree tops. The men were awakened by the splashing of water and the anguishing cries from a large black bear. The bear was approximately four hundred feet from their campsite. The bear had wandered into the lake to quench his thirst. Both men watched in amazement as small fish jumped out of the water and tore bits of flesh and hair from the bear's body. Jim and Bob ran over to the bear to get a better look at was happening to him.

Before they could reach the bear, he was gone from sight. The water had turned a crimson red in color.

"My God... he's gone!" exclaimed Jim. "Those fish stripped him of all his flesh in just a matter of minutes. What kind of fish could do a thing like that?"

Bob Graves paused a moment, "Piranha," he said quietly. They watched the water change from the crimson color, back to its natural bluish green color. The bears stripped skeleton bones laid submerged in three feet of murky water.

The two men walked back to their campsite without uttering a single word. Jim was sickened by the thought that it could have been him laying on the bottom of the lake had he gotten into the water to swim and tow the airplane.

They consumed that last of their food supply for breakfast. The remainder of the day was spent in trying to repair the damage to the airplane. They found some dried tree bark lying on the ground. They were able to use it to patch the holes in both the elevator and fuselage. A length of cable wire, attached to one of the plane's seats, was used to connect the controls for the elevator.

"Boy, I'm famished," said Jim. "Why don't we split up and try to find some fruit or berries to eat?" Bob agreed to the suggestion. Two minutes later, they went in opposite directions to find the food.

After wandering for some time, Bob was finally successful in locating several wild berry bushes and other wild fruit growing on trees.

Jim trudged his way through thick undergrowth. He searched for an hour with no luck in finding any eatable food.

A voice called out to him from the distance. It was a very strange sounding voice. It didn't sound like Bob's voice. It was more like a woman's voice. Jim headed in the direction that he thought the voice came from.

Traveling a few more minutes, he exited the heavy underbrush and found himself standing at the edge of a large clearing. The sight was beholding. Various flowers and an abundance of fruit grew everywhere.

"There's plenty of food here for us to eat," Jim mumbled to himself. He had momentarily forgotten about the strange voice that he had heard. There was really something strange and unusual about this place. A large weeping willow tree bore multiple fruit on its branches - - bananas - - apples and peaches. Strawberries, blackberries and blueberries all grew together on the same bushes.

This can't be real, thought Jim. I have to be dreaming. He walked over to one of the trees and touched the fruit. They were real. He yanked a peach from one of the branches and bit into it. It tasted cool, sweet and delicious.

Jim thought, in this strange place, it could be that these strange things that I see are normal? What a discovery. To have a plant that can produce three different types of fruit, all at the same time. I'll take some tree samples back with me. I'll make a fortune. *"I'LL BE RICH,"* he mumbled aloud.

As Jim was consuming more of the fruit, he heard the strange voice again. He turned. Standing at the opposite end of the clearing was the image of the most beautiful dark skinned native woman that he had ever seen. She was wearing nothing but what nature had given her. Her arms were extended outward, beckoning for Jim to come to her.

What's a woman like that doing here? He thought. Again the image beckoned for Jim to come closer. He had to investigate this strange phenomenon. Maybe the woman could answer some of his questions about this place?

Jim approached the center of the clearing. The ground beneath his feet seemed to be erupting. He lost his balance and fell to the ground. A giant green, sticky leaf wrapped itself around Jim's ankle. He looked around the clearing for help. The woman, along with all the flowers, fruit and berries, had disappeared.

The entire area had turned into a haven for carnivorous plants. The realization had finally struck Jim. Everything that he had seen was just an hallucination. A clever and devious way for the plants to lure their prey into their dens of death. Nothing was real. Even the bunch of bananas that he held in his hand had turned into a cluster of moving leaves.

"I'VE BEEN TRICKED," screamed Jim.

He felt himself slowly being dragged into the center of the plant. The plant that held him captive was twice as big as the surrounding plants. Upon reaching the center of the plant, Jim managed to stand up. He tried to break free from the plants grasp. His efforts were useless. More of the giant plant's leaves wrapped themselves around Jim's body. A white sticky substance oozed from the pores of the large pod. The fluid slowly covered Jim's feet... then his ankles. He tried to free himself again. It was totally useless. He felt a burning sensation in both of his feet. The pain was unbearable. Jim screamed in total agony.

Bob heard his partner's screams of pain. He followed them directly to the clearing. He watched in horror as the giant leaves engulfed Jim's entire body.

"*JIM...JIM!*" he screamed. Only Jim's head was exposed. He shouted, "*BOB, STAY BACK. THEY'RE CARNIVOROUS PLANTS.*"

"*HOLD ON, JIM,*" Bob shouted as he ran towards the giant plant. "*I'LL GET YOU OUT, SOMEHOW.*" Using the ax that he held in his hand, Bob hacked his way to Jim. Each swing was a cut into a giant leaf. Red crimson fluid oozed from the deep gashes.

"*THEY'RE ALMOST HUMAN,*" Bob screamed as he swung his ax. Within minutes, Bob reached the plant that was devouring Jim's body. He began swinging his ax at the base of the giant plant. More red fluid poured out from each slice that Bob made with his ax. At last, Jim was free of the plants grasp.

Jim couldn't stand the pain anymore. He passed out. Bob dragged Jim's limp body to the edge of the clearing. He looked down at Jim's legs. Both of his feet, up to the ankles, were missing. The plant had secreted an acid that dissolved both skin and bone. Jim was bleeding badly. Bob tied a tourniquet around each of Jim's legs. He succeeded in stopping the bleeding , but not in its entirety. Blood still oozed from the stumps that once were Jim's feet.

Bob lifted his partner and draped him over his shoulder. He struggled, trying to get back to their campsite. The dripping blood, from Jim's feet, mapped out the trail back to their campsite. The giant plant had become obsessed from the taste of blood and flesh. It sent out its giant limbs, pursuing the trail of blood through the underbrush.

V

Bob threw more wood on the fire. Only one thing to do, he thought, I've got to stop that bleeding. He put the ax head into the fire. Within minutes, the metal ax head was white hot. Bob picked up the ax and walked over to his partner. Jim was still unconscious. He cauterized each of Jim's feet with the white hot inferno. The bleeding stopped.

Suddenly, the quiet underbrush came alive with movement. A giant leaf vaulted forward and wrapped itself around Bob's waist. He swung the ax, hacking at the giant leaf until he was free of its grasp. His clothes were saturated with the red substance from the plant.

Bob picked Jim up and carried him back to their airplane. Bob opened the airplane's door. Jim started to come awake as he was placed in his seat. Bob left the plane and went back to the campsite to get his ax. Getting the ax was necessary to cut the rope and free the plane so they could take off.

As Bob Graves approached the campsite, giant green limbs came out of every part of the underbrush. He picked up the ax and started to run back to the airplane. Another giant leaf wrapped itself around Bob's ankle. He hacked at it with the ax until he was free. Bob made his way back to the plane and cut the rope anchoring the airplane to the two large oak trees.

He climbed into the pilot's seat, turned on the ignition switch, twisted the gasoline valve and pressed the starter button. The propeller turned slowly. The engine wouldn't start. Bob looked out of his side window. Giant green leaves and limbs had already started wrapping themselves around the pontoons. Bob pressed the starter button again. The engine started!

The propeller ripped and tore away the giant green leaf that had started wrapping itself around it. Red splotches covered the airplane's windows. Bob pulled out the trottel and pushed forward on the control stick. The airplane's engine labored as it tried to free itself from the giant leaves grasp. The power from the engine was to much for the giant leaves. The airplane lunged forward, breaking free, leaving pieces of the giant plant still attached to the sections of the tail and pontoons. The plane skimmed across the water. Finally, it lifted up into the air.

"*WE MADE IT, JIM... WE MADE IT*," Bob shouted.

The airplane circled the lake, slowly gaining altitude. Higher and higher it went until they finally reached five thousand feet.

"Free at last," said Bob. Without notice, the airplane developed an uncontrollable vibration. Bob tried to keep it level, but the airplane had become tail heavy. Bob looked out of his side window. The pieces of plant attached to the tail section had started to grow. Jim never uttered a word. He was going into shock.

"*THAT'S IT*," Bob shouted to Jim, "*OXYGEN STOPS THE PLANTS FROM GROWING AT AN ENORMOUS RATE. THAT'S WHY THE LAKE ISN'T OVERRUN WITH THOSE THINGS. I'VE STARTED THEM GROWING BY BRINGING THEM UP TO THIS ALTITUDE.*"

Loud scratching noises came from the floor below him. He guessed that the plants attached to the pontoons had started to grow too. Bob stared at Jim's bloody stumps. Small green buds had started to emerge from the stumps and started growing rapidly.

That's how the plants got started, thought Bob, from the blood and the flesh of a human being. I can't fly back to civilization with these plants hanging on to the plane.

Bob tried to give a distress call for the last time on the radio. It was useless. Jim screamed from the unbearable pain that was forced on him. As the plants grew and got heavier, the airplane lost altitude. Bob felt movement against his legs. He looked down at his feet. Tiny pieces of leaves, inside of the cuffs of his pants, were also growing. He knew what he had to do. "Sorry, Jim," he said softly, "I only hope the water will kill it." Bob Graves shut off the airplane engine, closed his eyes, crossed himself and pushed the control stick forward. The nose of the airplane faced downward.

ORDER FORM

Make checks payable to
Thomas E. Krupowicz

Mail To:
Terk Books & Publishers
P.O. Box 160
Palos Heights, IL 60463

Bill to:
Name _____
Title _____
Organization _____
Address _____
City _____ State _____
Zip _____
Purchase Order # _____

Ship to:
Name _____
Title _____
Organization _____
Address _____
City _____ State _____
Zip _____
Phone _____

Quantity	Title	Unit Price	Total
SUBTOTAL			
TAX: Illinois residents add 8.75% sales tax --unless exempt.			
S/H: $3.50 for 1st item. 50c each additional item.			
TOTAL AMOUNT			

TERK BOOKS